KEPT BY HIM

MEASHA STONE

Copyright © 2021 by Stormy Night Publications and Measha Stone

All rights reserved. No part of this book may be reproduced or transmitted in any form or by any means, electronic or mechanical, including photocopying, recording, or by any information storage and retrieval system, without permission in writing from the publisher.

Published by Stormy Night Publications and Design, LLC.
www.StormyNightPublications.com

Stone, Measha
Kept by Him

Cover Design by Korey Mae Johnson
Image by Shutterstock/HayDmitriy

This book is intended for *adults only*. Spanking and other sexual activities represented in this book are fantasies only, intended for adults.

CHAPTER 1

ena

Their laughter rolls over my skin like shards of glass. The clanking of coffee cups and dishes blasts like bombs in my ears.

"Lena, I told you not to drink that last shot," Marie chides me with a soft laugh. She shifts in her seat to help block some of the sun from pouring through the café window into my face. It doesn't help.

"I don't think it's that," I say, taking another sip of my coffee. My head hadn't ached when I woke this morning. It's only since I sat down with Marie and Tanya that a dull ache took root then bloomed into the thunderous pounding it is now.

"You look sort of pale," Tanya says, pressing the back of her hand to my cheek. "No fever."

I roll my eyes. "It's just a headache. A migraine probably. I haven't had one in a long time. I'm due." I brush her hand away. The alarm on my phone dings, and I check the time. "Shit. I'm going to be late." I down the rest of my latte in one large gulp.

"Off to the suburbs? Can't you stay a bit longer? We were going to go shopping." Marie tugs on my hand. A wave of nausea hits me, and I still myself for a moment until it fades. Maybe a trip out to my brother's house isn't such a good idea.

"Dom will murder me if I don't show," I say when I get moving again. Showing up with a migraine is better than not showing up at all. My oldest brother doesn't need another reason to lecture me on my perceived irresponsibility.

"Lena, you really look bad." Tanya stands from her chair. "Maybe I should drive you home."

"No. I'm fine." I sling my purse over my shoulder. The café is filled, not an empty seat to be had. I'm going to have to maneuver through the crowd to get to the door and every move I make brings another wave of unsteadiness.

"Are you sure?" Marie asks, concern weighing down the question. She glances over at the counter. "Let Sergio walk you to your car."

Sergio is her latest fuckbuddy. He'll do pretty much anything she asks if it means he'll get into her panties.

"No. No. It's too busy." I push her arm down. "It's just too crowded in here. I'll be fine once I get outside in the fresh air. Dominik's waiting and my father too. I'll be fine," I assure them, but the dark cloud fogging my head suggests I'm lying.

"What can I get you ladies?" Sergio pops up at our table, his eyes focused on Marie.

"Sergio, Lena's not feeling well. Will you take her to her car?" Marie lays on the sugar with her question.

"Sure." He turns to me. "You okay?"

"I'm fine." I roll my eyes, which sends my head into another spin. I grab hold of the back of my chair and take a deep breath. "It's all right."

He darts a look at the counter then back to me. "You sure?"

"Yeah. I'm good."

He nods, but his eyes are focused off in the distance, behind me.

"Okay, then. I should get back."

"I'll talk to you before I leave." Marie wiggles her fingers at him. He throws her a wink then hurries back between the tables. Sergio's family owns the Corner Café, a small café in the center of Chicago's Little Poland.

"I'll see you both tomorrow." I lean over and give Marie a peck to both cheeks then do the same with Tanya. "I need to give you the presents I brought back from Poland for you."

"Just be careful driving." Tanya squeezes me when she hugs me. "You really look bad."

I laugh, sending more pain through my head. "Thanks." I wave off her apology. I'm late, and my oldest brother will make me sit through a lecture I'm in no condition to sit through if I don't hurry.

Maneuvering through the café leaves me dizzy, but I don't stop moving until I'm outside. Taking a few deep breaths helps to settle my head. Maybe I'm nervous. My father has set the bar high for Dominik's wife, but he's impressed with her. If she's been able to tolerate Dominik for this long withing attempting his murder, I'm sure she's worth my father's approval. Standing beside her will probably only highlight my shortcomings.

My phone dings again with my notifications. I need to get going. I hurry across Milwaukee Avenue and head down the side street. Parking lots are a luxury this part of town doesn't have. I was lucky to find a spot on the street not too far from the café.

As I walk, another pair of footsteps falls in behind me. I slip my keys from my purse and tuck a single key between two of my fingers like Dominik taught me when I was in high school. My car is only two spots ahead of me.

My heart hammers into my ribs, falling in line with the heavy throb of my head.

I turn my head enough to see a single man walking. He's dressed in a pair of black jeans and a black t-shirt. His dark hair is slicked back across his head, and he's wearing a pair of sunglasses. He's catching up to me.

There's a bus stop on this corner. Maybe he's just trying to get to it before the next pickup.

Once I'm close, I click the unlock button on my fob and hurry to my door. I grab the door handle and look up. The man's gone.

As I pull the door toward me a hand smashes over my mouth from behind. I'm yanked backward into a hard chest. My mind whirls at the jerky movements. I can't catch my footing and my balance is gone.

"Keep quiet." The command is growled into my ear as I'm yanked toward the trunk of my car. I fling my arms, trying to catch him with my fingernails, but I'm losing strength. What was dizziness moments before has turned into a cyclone. My legs are heavy, my hands even more so.

Something's wrong with me. I'm not even fighting him as he pops the trunk and shoves me inside.

Once inside, I roll to my side, looking up at him. The man walking behind me. His glasses cover his eyes, but I can see the disgust curling his lip.

"Keep still." He points a finger at me. The sunlight from behind him blurs my vision. I push my hands again the trunk and try to sit, but my body rebels against me. I end up sinking down and laying my head against the pile of dry cleaning I was supposed to drop off yesterday but never did.

I close my eyes, but it's when the trunk is slammed that the darkness covers me. The car shifts. One door shuts then the other.

Two men speak. I can't hear them clearly. My head pounds harder, as though my brain wants out of my skull. I should be making the same noise against my trunk. I should be kicking and screaming, but it takes every ounce of energy I have to stay awake.

But even that only lasts another moment. The car's moving into traffic.

The men are still talking, and I realize why I can't understand them.

Lord help me.

These men are speaking Russian.

CHAPTER 2

*M*icah

The restaurant is alive. The wait staff gracefully whisks through the tables to the kitchen. Diners laugh and shovel food into their mouths between sips of expensive wine. As opening weekends go, this seems to be a success. I step out of the back office, tugging on my sleeve beneath my suit jacket.

A quick glance around the dining room and I find the reporter from the *Sun Times*. She's at a table with three other people, so I'll leave her alone. An honest review is what I'm after anyway. Getting in the way of her meal might work against me.

"Micah, don't forget your father," Niko, one of my most trusted men, tells me.

"I'm headed there now." I readjust my jacket before I make my way through the dining room to where he's enjoying his meal.

I stop a waitress, a little blonde thing with a round ass and generous tits. "Bring another bottle of wine to my father's table, and make sure he doesn't wait for anything. No delays. Understood?"

She bats her false eyelashes at me. "Of course, Mr. Ivanov."

I step into the back room where my father sits with my cousin, Dimitri. They've already enjoyed several appetizers; the empty platters are scattered around the table.

"Micah." My father's lips spread into a grin. He's been well fed, and the liquor has been pouring. He's in a good mood.

"Father." I shake his hand then turn to my cousin who is wiping his mouth with the white linen napkin. "Dimitri." I take the seat beside my father, pushing the place setting away from me.

"Everything so far is delicious." Dimitri pats his belly.

"Good to hear." The blonde waitress stops at the table with my drink—a shot of vodka with carbonated water. Good girl, I didn't even have to ask for it.

"Profits look good?" Money is my father, Roman Ivanov's, best friend.

I nod, assuring him the investment he made in the restaurant was a solid decision. "Once the reviews come out, we'll have a steady stream of customers. I already have the next two months' weekends booked for reservations," I explain.

"Good. Good." He nods. "We'll wait a few months and then we can talk about other options."

Laundering, he means.

"Six months at least," I say. In that time, I should be able to show him the profits that can be made with some legitimacy. Tainting the business with the Ivanov money won't benefit us, but it will take time to show him. My father is the head of our family, and it's been generations since we took a legitimate path. He's still married to the old ways, and it will take time.

"It would be nice if Igor were here, to see what you've done." My father gestures toward the crowded dining room. We're in a sectioned-off area of the restaurant but we can still see the majority of the restaurant.

"It would," I agree, averting my gaze to the floral centerpiece on the table. My older brother would have stopped me from even attempting this venture. Being the oldest, and next in line to take over our family line, he would have convinced my father what a foolish investment it was. Igor was powerful, strong, but he lacked vision that would move this family outside of the past.

Sadness flashes in my father's eyes at the mention of my older brother. Igor's been gone for two years, but in some ways my father mourns his death as though it happened yesterday.

"We see how well this place is doing, so, Dimitri. Tell me. How are you doing?" My father tears a piece of bread and chews on it. Business is a good cover for grief.

"Everything looks good on my end, Uncle." Dimitri runs his fingertips along the edge of his glass. "Profits will be up this month."

"Good, good."

I pluck the sliver of lime from the brim of my glass and drop it inside, swishing around the drink. This isn't the place for a business meeting, not with so many reporters in the restaurant. But telling Roman Ivanov what he can and can't do isn't my place.

"We can talk more in my office." I eye Dimitri then glance at my father. "Or at home."

"Here is fine." My father switches from English to Russian. "I have definitive proof of the Staszek family involvement in the lost shipment last month." My father's lips pinch together into a straight line.

Before I can question him, his meal arrives, and new plates are distributed. The house special of prime rib is put out before him. Another plate in front of Dimitri.

"Looks good." Dimitri picks up a fork and knife, ready to dig in. Once the servers are gone, I raise my brow at my father.

"You were saying?"

He leans back in his chair. "They stole the shipment."

"The entire lot?" I ask. There were over twenty women in the last shipment. I had warned him such a large group was risky, even with the help of the Garska family, but now isn't the time to remind him.

"What does Garska say about it?" I ask.

"Nothing." My father shakes his head. "He's dead. Shot in the head. Suicide." He wiggles his fingers in the air to project quotation marks.

"And you think Staszek had something to do with it? Wasn't he in Europe for a while? Legal trouble?" The Staszek family has held a truce with the Ivanov family for two decades.

They stay on their side of Chicago and we stay on ours. Everyone plays nice and stays alive. What would make them break the agreement now?

"He was, yes. His son, Dominik, took Garska's daughter for his wife. They intervened, took our girls."

Our girls.

My stomach knots at the phrasing. They're nothing more than product to my father. They were even less than that to my brother. To me, they're the guilt rotting my stomach. But I don't express my disgust for this part of his business—our business.

"Is Joseph Staszek home?" Maybe a conversation with the father will make the son fall in line. It's worked well enough in our family. But the Bratva men aren't easily swayed by our women. It will take a hell of a lot more than some girl to destroy my family name. If Dominik allowed his wife to get involved. If he did in fact steal my father's shipment of girls being sent home to Russia, the truce can be voided.

"He is." My father nods, digging his phone out of the inside of his pocket. He swipes across the screen several times then looks up at me with a severity I haven't seen since Igor's car was found wrapped around a traffic light. His eyes darken with a brewing storm, and his eyebrows, laced with traces of gray, knit together.

"This can't go unanswered, Micah." His words fall between us like concrete boulders. He considers the truce broken.

I steal a quick glance at my cousin, who salivates for a reason to go to war. He doesn't care about who, only that he'll be able to knock in heads, and kill his enemies without question or provocation. He's as savage as Igor was.

Not as cool-headed as me.

"What do you want done?" I lean one elbow on the table and turn toward him, giving him my full attention.

Plates clank in the dining room. A bubble of laughter bursts from somewhere near the bar. The restaurant can wait. I have managers to deal with the business. My father won't be placated like a toddler given a lollipop. He requires my utmost attention.

He turns his phone toward me. A photograph—no, a live stream.

"It's being taken care of."

CHAPTER 3

*L*ena

It's dark outside. Inside too.

There's a lamp on the side table beside the cot in this room I'm locked in, but I leave it off. I've seen enough of the white painted walls and cold cement flooring during the daytime. My headache is gone, as well as the nausea, leaving plenty of room for the breath-stealing fear to grow.

Whatever drug they laced my latte with has worked out of my system. Other than a dry mouth and hunger rumbling my stomach, I'm the picture of perfect health. There's a glass of water perched on the side table, next to the lamp, but I won't take the chance. Waking up in here was horrific enough the first time. If they drug me again, who knows where I'll wake up.

I clench my teeth together and wrap my arms around myself. The light sweater I was wearing over the thin cotton sundress when they took me does nothing to ward off the chill in this room.

Where am I?

I take another calm breath. Most of my energy is wasted on keeping calm. No one has spoken to me since I've been awake. Other than a small, frail woman rushing in with the water and then running back out, I've seen no one.

But they see me.

My attention focuses on the camera fixed to the ceiling in the corner of the room. The red light blinks at me, taunting me. Anyone could have taken me. My father isn't exactly well loved. A man with his power has enemies. It's how we ended up hiding out in Poland. Someone tried to have him arrested, put away for years if not the rest of his life. Now that they failed, they've taken me.

Crying from the other side of the door snags my attention and I rush to it, pressing my ear to the wood paneling. It's a thin door, one I could probably kick through. But it's also bolted.

"No! No!" A woman's plea scratches against me, sharp as glass. I yank on the handle again, cursing at the stupidity of it. I can't help that girl any more than I can help myself.

A door slams. More crying. A broken sob fades as the cries soften. She's been taken somewhere, but where?

The chill of the wood against my forehead as I press against it doesn't do anything to cool my anger. Or my fear.

I flatten my hands against the door, and count to ten as I drag in a breath. My diaphragm extends. Hold for three seconds, release. Repeat. On my third round, the bolt jiggles from the other side of the door.

Jerking backward, I barely miss being hit by it when it swings open. I trip on my heel, but catch myself before I fall on my ass by grabbing onto the edge of the bed.

The man in the doorway says nothing as he steps inside and shuts the door. What little light pouring in with him is blocked out again. He steps into a beam of moonlight spilling into the room from the small window.

He's well dressed in a suit. Leather shoes, firmly pressed black slacks. The white button-down shirt beneath his jacket has ivory buttons. He's missing a tie, and the top two buttons are open.

"Why don't you have the light on?" He breaks the suffocating silence.

I move around the bed, putting another foot between us. Somehow it matters, even though it doesn't.

"I don't need it." I keep my voice even. If he's the sort of monster that feeds off fear, he'll have to get his meal elsewhere.

His steps are quiet along the floor as he moves to the side table. With a click, yellow light floods the room. I close my eyes and look away for a moment, slowly letting them adjust. It's not bright, just new.

I blink my eyes open, bringing my attention into focus on him. My heart stops. Another second. It flutters to life again, dragging my lungs along with it.

I've seen this man before.

His dark hair is combed back, but not slick with gel as some of the other men I've seen him with. There's a shadow of a beard on his jaw, but it's the scar—jagged and long—that captures my gaze.

"Lena Staszek." My stomach twists as he says my name. "Your brother and your father have been very, very bad." He's taunting me.

"My brother and father are going to kill you when they find out what you've done," I threaten, and it's true. I'm a possession—their possession and they won't accept this insult.

He laughs. "Yes. I'm sure they'll want to." He scratches his jaw, along the scar. "Do you know where you are?" He levels his eyes on me. Danger. Every second his dark gaze focuses on me, my brain screams the word.

"You're an Ivanov," I accuse, not answering his question. I've seen the Ivanov family at parties, but I've never been so close.

Knowing who he is gives me insight to my location, but I'm not ready to admit it too loudly yet.

"Micah Ivanov." He slips his hands into his pockets. "I'll ask again, but this is the last time I'll be generous enough to repeat my question, do you know where you are?"

There's a warning underlining his words. My chest tightens. There is nowhere for me to run. If this man wants to do horrible, terrible things to me, I'll have nowhere to hide.

"I think so." I step further back until I'm pressed against the wall. It's not much, but at least it's some protection.

"Tell me," he insists, his chin raising a fraction. Is he daring me?

"This is where you hold the women you sell." My voice cracks on the last word, but I quickly clear my throat to cover it up. I've been told horror stories of the Ivanov family. The holding cells, the auctions, the trading of flesh.

"Yes." He pauses. "This is where my father holds the women he sells," he clarifies. There's a distinction he wants me to understand.

"I'm not one of those women," I tell him. "I'm Lena Staszek. My father, Joseph Staszek, will not stand for this. You should release me now before there's more trouble." I point to the door only two feet away to my right. He didn't lock it when he came in. I could throw it open and run—right into a guard.

"I know who you are." He smiles, as though this entire conversation is a playful distraction to the rest of his day. "I also know why you're here, but do you?"

"No." I drop my hand back to my side, fisting it.

"You're here because your family stole from mine." He folds his arms over his chest. "You're here as retribution for that theft. Though I'm not entirely sure we'll recoup the loss on your sale alone."

My sale.

My throat closes.

"You can't," I manage to say, pushing my chin higher. What my voice lacks in strength, I can make up in demeanor. My father always accused me of having a murderous glare when angered. I can only hope he wasn't exaggerating.

"Oh, I assure you we can."

"Whatever you think my father took from you, I promise you he didn't. There's a truce between our families. He wouldn't break that." I have no idea if I'm spewing lies or hope. Other than what I've overheard over the years, I know nothing of my father's true business dealings. As the youngest—and a girl—my father and brothers sheltered me from their work.

"Your father didn't, you're right. But your brother, Dominik, did." He glances at the cot. The sheets are wrinkled but otherwise undisturbed. "You haven't been sleeping."

"Let me call Dominik or my father. They'll sort this out," I offer.

His left eyebrow arches. "Do you really think that's going to happen?"

My shoulders drop. Of course it won't.

"They don't know where I am."

I had parked on a street with little pedestrian traffic. The odds that anyone saw what happened are slim. The odds that anyone would tell are even smaller. The Ivanovs aren't known for their generosity.

"Not yet. The video is being sent to him now." He points to the camera in the corner. "We'll see what the next step after that is."

"He won't let you sell me," I insist. He can't. My father may be many things, but he would never let them do such a thing to me. Not for any reason.

"We'll see." Micah shrugs then moves toward me. Already pressed against the wall, I have no escape. He picks up a long lock of my hair and rubs it between his two fingers. "There may be other options."

"There will be a war between our families. And my father will bring his allies to his aid," I school him.

His lips twist up into a satanic grin. "How many Polaks do you think he can gather?"

My body stiffens at the insult.

"Enough to end your family," I say, finding my strength again. I won't allow this asshole to look down on my family, on my people.

"You think so? You think your father will go to war over one girl?"

"I am his daughter." I lock gazes with him. He will not own me in this moment. I will not stand down to this Russian prick.

"True. But will the other families care once they find out the truce was broken by your brother and not my family?" He drops my hair and leans toward me. His warm breath rushes over my cheeks. "Do you think they'll care about poor little Lena wasting away in the Ivanov stable?"

"Fuck you." My insides rattle.

His eyes narrow, and he shakes his head. "We'll have to work on your attitude before the auction."

I clamp my mouth shut. Nothing I say will help my situation. He didn't come down here to talk with me; he's here to toy with me.

"I suggest you get some sleep, Lena. While you can." He runs the back of his knuckles over my cheek. "I'll be back tomorrow."

An icy tremor skates down my spine when he pulls back.

"I'll have food sent." He winks, then leaves me standing against the wall trembling.

Food? I won't eat it. I won't drink anything they send. And I won't sleep to give them an opportunity to mess with me. I will remain vigilant and find a way out of this mess.

I am a Staszek, and we don't give in to Russian scum.

CHAPTER 4

M icah

The girl has more grit to her than I would have given her credit for.

After giving the guards instructions to bring her a real meal, I went home. The stables leave a film on me that will take more than a shower to wash away. Igor built the bunker where the girls are kept. One of my father's prouder moments of my older brother.

It's going to be the first thing I destroy when my father hands the family over to me. But until that time, it remains and I do the only option open to me—nothing.

It's seven o'clock in the morning when my father rings me. "Staszek wants a meeting."

I stand at my bedroom window, sweat from my run already drying on my skin, and look down at the busy pedestrians rushing to work below. The penthouse condo where I live is far enough off the ground, city sounds don't rise up to me.

"How did you answer?"

"He'll be here tonight. Him and that fucking son of his."

"Do we know Dominik intervened knowing the shipment was on its way to our holdings in Moscow?"

"Does it matter?" he scoffs over the phone. It does to me, but I'm the reasonable one in our family. I'm the one who looks at the entire situation. Unlike him, I don't chase after immediate gratification with blinders on for the future.

"If we are going to file a grievance, I think we should know everything first." I dance at the edge of being helpful and lecturing. Igor would jump on this wagon with him, guns blazing ready to fight.

"Either way, the shipment was taken by the Staszek family. And for that, they lose their precious cargo."

"You're really going to sell that?" I raise my eyebrows.

"Of course I am. Or I can get rid of it? Which do you think would hurt them more?" He's like a wolf salivating over a fresh kill.

He doesn't need to elaborate, and it's best he not. Our phones are checked constantly, but they can still be tapped. People could be listening.

I shouldn't be hesitant. I shouldn't give a shit what happens to the Staszek girl.

"How much do you want to hurt them?" I turn away from my window and the bustle of life happening outside it. In another life I thought I'd be one of them. Running down the street, briefcase in hand, chasing after one deal or another. I'm still a businessman, but there's not much chasing happening. Deals are brokered differently in my world.

"This is more than a theft," my father says.

"It's about disrespect." I sum up the lecture for him before he can get started. I have shit to do and this call is taking up too much of my morning. "Where's the meeting?"

"I'll get the location to you later this morning."

"If the product is going to be shown, it will need some spit and polish first, I think."

My father disagrees. "Let them see what becomes of it when it stays in our possession."

His aim isn't to simply prance the girl around her family, but to enrage them. A war is going to erupt the moment that girl shows up dirty from the cell we've kept her in. I know how my family would react to such a display, and the Staszek family isn't so different than my own.

"If they see a damaged product, the meeting might turn hostile."

"Good reason to be well prepared then. I'll send you the details. I expect you there, Micah." As his second in command, I would be nowhere else.

"Of course." I make my way to the bathroom. I need a shower and a change of clothes. "I'll be there."

"Good. I can count on you. I know it." Does he though? There's a bit of hesitation in his tone, the same he's had ever since Igor's death.

"I'll see you later." I wait for him to hang up before I drop my phone on the counter and strip out of my clothes.

* * *

The house is quiet when I arrive at my father's house. By the heavy scent in the air, I've missed dinner. As I pass the dining room, I peek to be sure. It's empty, save for the kitchen staff clearing away the leftover food.

"Micah." Katarina, the housekeeper, smiles warmly when she notices my arrival. "You missed dinner, but I can make you a plate?" she offers.

"No, no, thank you," I say, glancing down the hall. "Is my father in his office?"

"Yes. He's expecting you."

"There are other men coming too." I glance at the ornamental clock hanging on the wall above the buffet. "Soon."

"Yes. When they arrive, I'll bring them straight to the office." She averts her eyes for a moment. "And then I'll be going home for the evening."

Katarina has worked for my family for as long as I can remember. She has no illusions about her job, about who she works for, but still escorting dangerous men to secret meetings puts her ill at ease. Even so, she's never hinted at leaving her post.

"Sounds good, Katarina." I start to walk off then pause. "Do you think you could wrap up a plate for me?"

I haven't gotten around to hiring a full staff, and whatever my housekeeper has made will most likely be as inedible as the other meals she's made. Katarina's cooking is home to me.

She smiles, a light flickers in her eyes. "Of course."

I give her a curt nod, then leave her to her work and head to my father's office.

Two soldiers stand outside his office and step aside as I pass them and go inside. Niko paces the room, probably contemplating my father's rage when he finds out what I've done.

"Micah. Good." My father checks his watch. "They should be here any minute." He turns to Niko. "I want the girl ready to be brought in, I don't want to have to wait."

"She's ready. Just down the hall. I'll get her myself when you're ready."

He's satisfied for the moment. "Good."

"I want to talk to you about this plan before they get here." I move to the bar in the corner of the room and pour myself a drink.

"What plan? We dangle the bitch in front of their faces."

Since my back is to him and he can't see me, I close my eyes and take a moment for my patience to fill. My father has carried the burden of keeping the Ivanov family at the top of the heap for so long, he's forgotten how hard he had to fight to get us here. Arrogance is a sure way to lose everything. And he's forgotten.

"And then what?" I turn on my heel and walk back to the desk, cradling the drink in my right hand. "They see her, get pissed, and then we have a pissing contest? What do you want from them? What can they offer that will make the truce valid again?"

His eyes narrow; wrinkles form around his eyes. "Truce? I don't want a fucking truce. I want their territory. We make good money on the girls, but if we cut into their drug trade, we'd double our money."

"Those territory lines were drawn long ago," I remind him.

"And if they want their precious daughter to avoid the auction block, they'll redraw them," he spouts at me.

It won't be hard. From what my sources have told me, Joseph Staszek dotes on his daughter like royalty. She's been spoiled her entire life, needing to only glance in the direction of a bauble before her father has purchased it and handed it to her with big fucking bow on top. If my father asks for a few more blocks of the city, Joseph Staszek will give it.

"You'll take more territory and hand the girl back over to them." I swirl the drink in my glass.

He looks to Niko then back at me. "She's precious to Joseph. He'll give up a large portion for her. Or he won't get her back." He shrugs like it doesn't matter to him which way it turns out. Like keeping her won't cause a war between our families that will drag out and kill our men.

"You kidnapped his daughter." I emphasize the reality, but he continues to look at me with his eyebrows drawn together. "He will want retribution for that."

Roman throws his hand in the air. "His fucking son stole my product! And I learned today, the train yard has been taken out of our control. We will need to find another way to move the girls. A more expensive way."

I sip my drink, letting the burn of the alcohol replace the sense of dread crawling up my chest. If they've cut us off from transportation, it's going to take more than a few blocks of territory to appease Roman.

A knock on the door cuts me off before I can speak. One of the soldiers' head peeks in.

"Sir. Staszek is here."

"Did you search him?" my father asks loudly, more for Joseph's sake than his own.

"Both are clean." The soldier nods.

"Let them in." My father gets out of his chair and leans forward with his knuckled fists on the desk.

I place my glass on the desk and move to stand beside my father. Niko rounds the desk and flanks him on the other side. United, we wait for the Staszeks to come claim what they believe to be theirs.

But I know how this will play out.

Lena Staszek won't be going home with her family tonight.

CHAPTER 5

ena

Leaning against an armchair, I suck in a deep breath. I close my eyes, count to three, breathe out slow. Repeat.

It's not working. My nerves shake, my stomach clenches, and my lungs aren't cooperating.

No one will tell me what was happening, or where I've been moved. A man came into my cell hours ago and pulled me from the underground bunker. He dragged me up into the bright sunlit afternoon, only to shove me into a car after yanking a cloth bag over my head. Did he think I would memorize my way back home?

The drive had been short, or at least it felt that way, and then I was dragged from the car and shoved into a house. I was allowed to shower, a relatively short reprieve. As soon as I was done, I was pulled this way and that until my hair was dried and brushed, fresh makeup applied to my face, and I was shoved into a short, tight-fitting black cocktail dress.

The neckline dips far between my breasts. I pull at it in an attempt to cover the swell of my breasts, but it's not helping.

And now, I'm waiting. For what? I have no fucking clue.

I drag in another breath, do the breathing, calm my heart, get air in, get air out. It should calm me.

It doesn't.

I've been in this room for over an hour. I'm not entirely sure what day it is, but there's a clock on the wall in here so at least I know what time it is. My stomach growls, but I push the hunger pangs from my mind. If I were to eat right now, I doubt it would stay down.

I grit my teeth. I am not this weak. I must be strong. No matter what these men want from me, I will not give it to them.

Anticipation of the unknown drives my racing heart. Once I'm in the thick of it, I'll regain composure. I'll be able to see the situation and find the way out. I just need to survive until whatever is about to happen actually does.

The door opens, and a man steps in. I recognize him from earlier. He brought me to this room and told me to wait.

"Let's go." He waves his hand at me to follow him.

"Where?" I question him. For all I know, he's taking me to my execution. Or worse, an auction block.

His shoulders drop. "Just come. And when we get there, don't speak. Not a fucking word, do you understand?" He grabs hold of my elbow when I get close enough and tows me along the hallway.

I'm too busy watching where he's taking me to notice much about the house, other than a woman scurrying out of the hallway when we approach. Would she even help me if I cried out to her?

He turns down another corridor and we walk down the long walkway to a closed door. Two more men stand guarding the door. I swallow back another question.

"Not a word," he reminds me, then pushes the door open and shoves me forward ahead of him.

"Lena!" My father's voice yanks my attention. Relief floods me. He's here. Next to him, my oldest brother, Dominik. They've come for me.

As I take a step in their direction, my escort grabs hold of my arm again and pulls me back. I try to yank free, but his nails dig into my skin.

"Let her go," Dominik orders, but my escort doesn't seem to understand Dominik's not used to repeating himself. He pulls me further to the side, away from them.

"Now you've seen her," the man standing behind the desk says. His eyes widen just a fraction when his gaze sweeps over me, like he expected something or someone else.

"Lena, are you all right? Are you hurt?" my father asks, keeping his voice firm. His eyes bore into me, trying to find the truth in my gaze, but he must pretend that he's not panicking. He's not upset by his daughter standing in this office, a captive of a rival family.

"I'm all right." I yank my arm out of my escort's grip and fold my hands in front of myself. Everything is going to work out fine now. I just need to let Dominik and my father do what they do best.

I raise my chin and settle in to listen to their conversation. They'll negotiate and I'll be home and in my bed in a matter of hours.

My gaze settles on the other man in the room. The man who came into my cell yesterday to scare me. His dark glare sends a shiver down my spine. His hands are in his pockets, his jaw set firm.

I swallow, wetting my dry throat and tear my gaze from him. He's unsettling, but I'll be away from him soon enough.

"You are lucky she hasn't been mistreated." Dominik's voice tears through my thoughts. Mistreated? I've been pissing in a bucket but telling him that now will only stall progress.

"You can't think to keep her. I won't allow it." My father fists his hand and shakes it. "We have a fucking truce, Roman."

"Yes. We did." Roman leans forward on his knuckles, his face red, eyes bulging. "We fucking did and then you interrupted my shipment. Took my girls, and now have blocked my transport."

"We had no way of knowing that shipment belonged to you," Dominik argues.

"If you had, would you have left it alone?" Micah speaks, focusing his attention on my brother. "If you had no problem taking over the shipment from your wife's own father, I have trouble believing you'd have walked away once you became aware it belonged to us."

Dominik's jaw ticks.

My father clears his throat, and a hot trail of anxiety runs through my veins. It's a signal.

"What's done is done. We weren't aware of your involvement. But we are now." My father glances over at me; a sadness tints his eyes but is drowned out by stern resolve.

My chest tightens. I'm not part of this. None of this has anything to do with me, but I'm going to bear the brunt of the consequences.

You'll be a good girl and do what's expected of you.

In a flash I recall my father's words. We'd been talking about my future, or rather I'd been trying to talk about it. He wouldn't engage, he merely made that one statement.

You'll be a good girl and do what's expected of you, Lena.

"Let's come to an agreement and put this mess behind us. We've spent many years with peace, and both of our families have prospered. Let's not ruin that over one mishap." My father's diplomacy isn't going to work. Roman Ivanov has a gleam in his eye that reeks of victory. My father is ready to make concessions, and Roman is going to strike.

No sooner does my foot move forward than the guard grabs my elbow and pulls me back. I'm to stand and watch but not participate. Have they all forgotten that it was me who was kidnapped? Drugged and stuffed in my own trunk?

"Your daughter is beautiful. I could probably get more for her on the market than the entire lot you took." Roman keeps his steady gaze fixated on my father.

Dominik shows no outward reaction, but I know my brother. He's only waiting for my father's signal and then he'll pounce. He won't allow this to happen to me. This is his fault. He put our family in this position.

"You would go to war over one fucking mistake?" My father's eyes narrow, his voice lowers. He's had enough talk.

"I would go to war over your family stealing from me. This truce has never brought both of us equal profits."

My father's nostrils flare and he fists his hands at his sides. "I'm willing to repay your loss on the shipment. You'll have access to the trains again, we can both use the train yard as a port, neither of us needs to choke out the other."

Roman runs his tongue over his top teeth from beneath his lip.

A brush of heat floods my face, and when I look, I find Micah staring at me again. He doesn't bother pretending to consider my father's offer, not like Roman. Micah remains as confident and unmoving as before. It's like he already knows the outcome of this meeting and doesn't feel the need to pay attention.

"And retribution for your daughter's stay with us?" Roman asks in a low tone.

"As long as she leaves with us tonight, there will be none," my father decides.

They will go unpunished. Nothing will happen to these men who abducted me and treated me like a scrap of garbage to be left in the cell underground.

Because I'm a woman and must do what's right for the entire family, not just for myself. My chest grows heavy beneath their words and the consequences of them.

Roman taps his chin with his middle finger. "I have another idea. She'll stay with us. One woman in exchange for the twenty you took."

"No." I jerk free of the hold on my arm and step forward. "I'm not staying here. I won't let you sell me." I turn to my father. "Do something. You can't think to go along with this." Desperation takes hold, making me sound like the spoiled brat outsiders believe me to be.

We are in the Ivanov mansion. They could walk in and gun us all down. My father had to have known that; why would he agree to meeting here of all places?

"I won't let you take her." My father ignores me and speaks directly to Roman.

"No, of course not," Roman agrees, leaning forward again. "A marriage. Between your daughter and my son. As a way to seal our truce once more. Bring peace back."

"What?" I rush toward my father, but my guard grabs me again. One hard look from Dominik, and he lets me go. "Absolutely not."

My father doesn't glance at me, doesn't acknowledge my words.

"Daddy," I whisper. When I was a little girl, I would claw at my father's pant leg to get his attention. I doubt it would work now. His concrete stare is fixated elsewhere. He's tuned me out.

"Give me a moment to talk to my daughter."

My heart drops.

"There's nothing to talk about. I won't do it." I turn toward Micah who has a hint of amusement tugging on his lips. "I won't marry you. This is absurd. I have nothing to do with any of this."

"We'll let you have the room for a few moments." Micah's glare turns from me to my father as he speaks.

I'm in a nightmare. No one understands what I'm saying, they can't hear me, or they don't care. It's like I'm not in the room. The air thickens and by the time the door closes behind the three Ivanov men, I'm gasping for it.

"Lena, calm down," my father chastises me softly. I take a shaky breath, trying to force the panic in my chest to ease off.

"I won't do this. How can you even think it?" I ask. "They kidnapped me, threw me in a trunk, drugged me. Left me in a cold cell with a bucket for a bathroom and now you want me to marry one of them?" I've never learned how to keep the tremor from my voice.

"Lena." Dominik's hard voice grabs my attention. When I look up at him, I see the remorse in his eyes. He's going along with this crazy idea. "It will bring peace. Many of Garska's men have fled the city. Only a few of them joined us. We were able to get the charges dropped against Dad, but we're still being watched. If the Ivanov family attack, it's more dangerous for us to retaliate, to defend."

I know he's right, and Roman Ivanov knows it too. Why else would he offer such a thing?

"You knew, Lena, that one day you would marry for the good of the family. I've never held that fact from you. Just like your brother did." My father gestures toward Dominik.

"It's because of *his marriage* this is happening to me." I turn my anger on my big brother. "You couldn't tell your wife no?

You couldn't take one fucking minute to realize what could happen by stopping that shipment?"

Dominik's eyes darken. I'm standing on the line; one more word and I'll be over it. But I don't care.

"Give them Kasia. She's the one who fucked up their shipment. Give them her."

"How can you say such a thing?" My father's admonishment hits me in the chest. He'd protect Dominik's wife over me? I'm his daughter. I'm the one who was dragged to Poland while he was waiting out his legal trouble here in Chicago.

"How can you consider making me marry that man!" Tears burn my eyes. I'm climbing uphill in stilettos with a fifty-pound rucksack. This is not a battle I'm going to win. Not when my own family sides with the enemy.

"I've heard things about Micah." My father switches to Polish. These walls have ears and up until now, he hasn't said anything worth hearing. "He's not as stupid as his father. He sees everything and makes calculated decisions."

"What does that have to do with anything?" I don't care how well he manages his family. It's my life I'm struggling to save here, and I'm losing my grip on it.

"When he gains full power in his family, you'll be married to the head of the Ivanov family. As much as I hate the fucking Russian pricks, there is strength in that. You will be protected. Our family will be protected. If we don't do this, it will be a war. And you'll be a target."

My insides shake. He's not only allowing this, he sees opportunity within this deal. At handing me over to the monsters.

"Don't make me do this." I lower my gaze, unable to stand another moment of my brother or my father looking at me. All the years they pretended I was precious to them, loved and cared for, it was all bullshit.

It was all an act.

They tended to me as if to fatten the lamb before bringing it to slaughter.

The door opens and the Ivanov men are back, blocking the doorway.

"Your answer," Roman demands.

A hot tear rolls down my cheek, and I turn away, so the Ivanov scum don't have a chance to enjoy it.

My father grasps my hands, squeezing gently as if to give me some of his strength.

"A marriage between our families is agreed." He drops my hands, and I take a shuddering breath.

In a heartbeat my entire future is whisked away beyond my grasp.

CHAPTER 6

*M*_{icah}

Color drains from Lena's cheeks as she sits quietly between her brother and her father while the details of the deal are worked out. She doesn't raise her gaze from the edge of my father's desk. My father will see this as a sign of obedience. A woman who knows her place among men, silent and waiting for direction.

Her thumbnail jams beneath the manicured nail of her opposite hand. She drags it beneath each nail until she gets to the pinky, and then starts again with her thumb. This isn't an obedient woman; this is a woman biding her time. How many ways has she killed us in her mind?

"We'll bring her home tonight—"

"No." I push off the edge of the desk where I'm leaning. "I think it's safer for her to stay with me." I level Joseph Staszek with a glare, daring him to deny me. Dominik can bluster all he wants, he's in the same position as me. Until his father relinquishes full control, he will have to follow orders—same as me.

"The wedding. When will it take place?" Joseph asks, turning his gaze back to my father, dismissing me.

"Sooner the better," my father says with a shrug. "A week."

"A week?" Lena's eyes dart up to my father, her eyebrows rise beneath her trimmed bangs.

"A week," my father says with more confidence. Her unease fuels him. She should learn from that if she's to survive my family.

Wife or not, she will be expected to behave a certain way.

Wife. My mind still hasn't absorbed the concept. Roman gave me no indication he had even considered the possibility. While we stepped into the next room for the Staszek men to reel Lena into cooperating, he gave me no explanation. I didn't need one. Marriage to her or marriage to any other woman was the same to me.

Men in my position don't search out love. We sure as hell don't date. If I wanted the company of a woman, I had plenty to choose from, but they weren't long arrangements. I never made promises, and they never held expectations from a man like me.

But looking at Lena when her father made the agreement, seeing the hope drain from her eyes lit a fire beneath my skin. Maybe she didn't understand her position. Daughter to a mob boss, Polish or not, would be expected to marry at the advantage of her father if necessary. And after what her brother pulled, it became necessary.

The meeting finally ends past eleven o'clock. Lena sits in the same chair, her shoulders bowed forward. I wonder if she's slept at all while down in the stables. I had told her to get rest, but I doubt she would have given my orders any weight.

"Niko, take Lena to the car. I'll be there soon."

"Now?" Lena leaps to her feet, searching out her father for protection that he's not going to offer. Instead, he slowly clamps his mouth closed and gives her a curt nod.

"I'll come to see you, Dominik and Jakub, too," he says to her in Polish. They don't think I speak their language, and I won't let on that I do yet.

Dominik looks at her. This is his fault, and by the tinge of darkness in his eyes he knows it. "I can bring Kasia if you'd like."

At this, her jaw clenches and a sharp redness covers her cheeks. "Don't bring that woman near me." She turns on her heel, marching past Niko and through the office door without another word. I won't take offense that she didn't bother to look my way before departing, but I will explain manners to her later on.

The click of her heels on the marble flooring in the hallway fades as Niko leads her from the house. Dominik steps up to me as his father and mine say their goodbyes. He scans me with a hot glare I'm sure has more to do with him being her oldest brother than his distaste for me.

"If you hurt her—" The threat dies in the air between us. Yes, this is the big brother protecting his little sister. I'll let him bang his chest for now. I'm feeling generous.

"No more than I have to," I say with a wink and his jaw clenches. He gets my meaning. "You worry too much,

Staszek. We've just created peace. Why would I do anything to fuck that up? It's a good thing. Only a fool would play around with such a deal."

My comment hits the mark, and his eyes narrow. I pick up my glass from the desk where it's sat throughout the meeting, and down the last bit while keeping my gaze locked on his.

"Dominik. Let's go," Joseph barks at his son and shuffles toward the exit. Dominik's jaw ticks. He's fighting back words that will make matters worse.

With another glance at my father, Dominik follows his father from the room, slamming the door behind them hard enough the door shakes.

"Well," my father groans as he sits back in his chair. The arthritis in his knees hurts him by the end of the day, and with all the tension of the last few hours, I'm sure he'll be sore throughout the night. "That went better than I thought." He rubs his chin. "I should have thought of marriage before."

"Maybe you could have run it past me first, then." I bring my empty glass back to the bar and pour two more fingers of vodka.

"Why? You do what's best for the family."

He's not wrong. "Still. Some warning would have been appreciated," I say then shoot back the liquor. The heat crawling down my throat and spreading through my chest is welcomed after the tension of the night.

"You let that girl shower and put her in a nice dress. You even had someone come in to do her hair and put that awful makeup on her, didn't you?"

"I did." I slide my hands into my pockets. "Do you think Joseph would have been so easy to maneuver if he was raging over the treatment of his little girl? Boss or not, she is his daughter and any disrespect you showed her would have made this meeting more dangerous. For all of us."

He stares at me for a long moment then pinches his lips together and concedes the point. "You're right. It went better this way. Good call, Micah."

"What's your angle with this marriage?" A day ago he wanted this girl sold to the highest bidder, even contemplating killing her to hurt the Staszeks. Now he wants to fold her into our family?

"Angle?" He laughs. "You saw Joseph. It was killing him to see her in my office. Under my control. He knows this is his fault and, in a war, he'd lose more than he'd win. He broke the truce, by accident yes, but still his fault. He has to make it right. Now, he'll pay for the girls he stole, and we get to keep his daughter. Parade her around as one of our own. Fill her belly with our family genes. What better humiliation is there than that?"

"And the girl?" I ask, sure I know the answer.

"Who cares. She'll do what she's told." He points a finger at me. "I expect you to keep her in line. She may take your name and give you children, but she's still a Staszek whore."

The picture becomes clearer now. For once my father has thought ahead. He's not looking to make a truce; he's looking to embarrass the Staszek family. To provoke them.

"Any abuse of her will give them cause to break the truce, and it will be our doing," I remind him.

He waves a hand through the air. "I'm not suggesting you beat the woman. But you make her understand her place in this family. She'll do what she's told. She won't cause trouble, and she'll give you sons."

I put the empty glass on the desk. "I'll take care of it."

"I know you will," he says, but I don't miss the clear warning in his voice. If I don't handle this the way he wants, he'll be sure to take care of things himself.

I leave him in his office without another word. He's already made it clear what he wants. Anything from me that doesn't support him will insult him.

When I step out onto the front porch, I see my car idling a short distance on the driveway. Niko is in the front seat, and my fiancée is sitting in the back, staring out the other side into the darkness.

I wonder if she understands her luck. Any other turn of events and she'd be heading back to the stables.

Instead, she's being taken home with me.

Lucky girl.

CHAPTER 7

ena

I'm lucky on the drive from Roman's house. Micah sits up front with his henchmen and doesn't try to talk to me.

The silence gives me a chance to consider my options. Running away would mean staying on the run and not speaking to my family again. At least for a lengthy period of time. They would deserve it, my father and my brothers. Though maybe I can't fault Jakub. Or maybe I can. He didn't exactly barge into the meeting to help me.

The darkness of the night sky doesn't stop the city lights from illuminating our way down Michigan Avenue. Roman Ivanov lives in an estate, protected by steel gates. My fiancé likes the city apparently.

The SUV pulls into a parking garage and the bright lights wash over the car as we drive up the ramp to a private spot.

My car door is opened for me and I scoot out, ignoring the hand being offered. Micah cups my elbow and pulls me toward the elevators.

He still hasn't spoken a word to me. When we approach the elevator, he jams his finger into the call button then turns to Niko.

They have a rapid conversation in Russian. I know a few words, but they speak too quickly for me to catch them all in the right order. When they're done, Niko goes back to the SUV, leaving us alone as the elevator doors slide open.

This is it. If I step into this little box, I'll never be allowed out.

"Don't be difficult, Lena." He steps into the elevator, turns and faces me. There's a daring in his eyes, like he almost hopes I give him trouble.

I force my gaze to meet his, taking in his dark eyes, and step into the elevator with him. I catch a whiff of his aftershave when he reaches around me to hit the buttons on the panel in front of me. It's a warm scent, spicy.

He presses the penthouse button then puts in his code and the elevator doors ease closed. We're trapped in this little box together. Alone.

"You did good tonight," he says from behind me. I raise my eyes to the lights checking off the floors overhead and say nothing.

Did good. I've gone from one prison to another, how is that progress?

Little hairs on the back of my neck tingle as they rise. I won't look, I won't give him the satisfaction of glancing over my shoulder at him. I flatten my hands against my stomach, pulling each breath in through my nose and releasing it through my mouth. No matter how many breaths I take, I can't shake off his stare from behind me.

I must look such a fool to him. A girl easily stolen from the street. A daughter completely dispensable to her family.

The elevator dings, signaling we've arrived at the top floor of the high-rise, but the doors don't open. Before I can hit the open-door button, Micah reaches around me again. His chin brushes against my shoulder as he punches in another code. The red flashing light above the panel turns green and the doors slide open, revealing the penthouse waiting for us.

"Is that really safe?" I ask, stepping off the elevator into the pristine foyer. White and gray marble flooring spreads out across the round foyer and drifts off down the long corridor. A round mahogany table sits in the middle of the entrance way with a large crystal vase filled with a colorful flower arrangement. A simple chandelier of white iron and candle-shaped lights dangles over the arrangement.

"No one can enter without the code." He waits for the elevator to close and puts in another code into the keypad on the inside of the penthouse. "And now, no one can leave without it."

An opportunity missed; I should have watched him punching in the numbers.

"Follow me," he says and takes off down the corridor in front of us. There are hallways leading off the foyer to the right and left as well, but I follow him instead of exploring on my own. His leather-soled shoes clap against the flooring between the clicks my heels make as I follow him.

"Living room to the right, family room to the left." He points toward the rooms as we pass them. I only have time for a quick glance. A magazine could be shot here, the decor is so crisp and modern.

"That's the dining room." He gestures toward his right then nods to the left. "The guest bedroom."

The wide hallway acts as the vein of the residence with the room being offshoots. Micah takes a sharp turn down a hallway on his right, and I stumble in my footing to keep up with him.

"It's late," I say. "I think I'd like to just go to bed."

He makes another turn after we pass a closed door and I have to hurry to keep up with him, smacking right into his back. He's a solid wall; doesn't move a fraction. I grab hold of his suit jacket to keep from tumbling down.

"Whoa." He turns, grabbing my hands and helping me get on solid footing. "Careful."

I look at my hands, engulfed by his larger ones. If he were to squeeze hard enough, he could break my bones easily. And there would be no one to stop him.

Yanking my hands from his grip, I take a small step back.

"You'll eat something, then I'll take you to your room." He glances over me. "You didn't eat when I told you to before."

"I wasn't hungry." I raise my chin with my lie. I wouldn't have been able to keep it down if I had tried to eat anything. Being held captive by a sex trade family works against proper digestion.

He studies me for a long minute, like he's waiting for me to confess some big sin.

"I'm not all that hungry now either," I add.

"You can manage a sandwich." He moves to the refrigerator and points to the barstools on the other side of a kitchen island. The kitchen could double as a gourmet chef's playground.

I ease myself onto a barstool and tuck my hair behind my ears. It's been a long day, a longer evening, and my nerves have endured all they can for one day. A glass of red wine and a hot bath would help, but I won't ask. I'll simply take what he gives and when he shows me to my room, I'll sink into the bed and pray for sleep to consume me. Maybe when I wake up this will all have been a really weird dream.

"Hasn't anyone ever told you to lay low with your money?" I ask while he digs around the fridge. He turns back to me with a container of sliced ham and a plump red tomato. "This place is, well, amazing but doesn't it worry you? Won't it bring attention?"

He grabs a plate from the cabinet and begins putting together a sandwich.

"No," he answers after he's carefully placed the second slice of bread on the sandwich and slices it in half from corner to corner.

"No?"

"No," he says again and pushes the small plate across the countertop. "Eat."

I pick up one half of the sandwich and take a large bite. Turns out I'm famished and finish the entire sandwich while he watches me take every bite.

"That was good," I say, wiping my mouth with the napkin he hands me.

"Delphia is my housekeeper. She says she smoked the ham herself, but I think she gets it from a farmer out in the west suburbs where her family lives." He takes the plate from me and places it in the deep stainless-steel sink.

When he turns back to me, he presses his ass and his hands against the sink edge. He's taken off his suit jacket and tossed it on one of the barstools and loosened his tie. In this position he looks almost civil.

I jerk my gaze away from him. It's easier when he doesn't look so casual.

"You can walk away from this, you know," I say, keeping my eyes away from his. If I look into the darkness of his gaze, he'll suck me in. I can feel it inside me, how easily I can get lost there.

He's an Ivanov. A man I'm being forced to marry, I can't afford to lose myself to attraction. No matter how strong. I have to stay on my toes. Look for an angle that will wake me from this nightmare.

"I could," he agrees with me. "But I think both of our fathers would take issue with that."

I roll my eyes and drop one foot to the floor. "Not a man of his own will then. I see."

He laughs at my attempt to insult his manhood. "I'm as tied to my family as you are to yours. There's no shame in that. There's honor in doing your duty by your family. To being loyal."

I flick a quick glance at him. "And was it loyal when my father bartered me away for peace?" There's a bite to my words that I can't hide.

"Your father does what's best for the whole family." His answer doesn't really answer me. Did I really expect anything else?

I slip from the stool. "I'd like to go to bed now." I put my finger up in the air. "Alone."

He lifts his left eyebrow. "And you think you have that right?"

"I'm not married to you yet."

"No, but you're still mine, Lena. Make no mistake about that. I don't need a priest to make that happen. Our fathers' agreement already did."

My stomach twists. He's right. The priest blessing our union is pure theatrics. As far as the families are concerned, we're together. I'm his.

"But I have a phone call to make. I'll take you to your room." He grabs his jacket from the stool where he deposited it and leads me from the kitchen. We backtrack down the small hallway to the main larger corridor and after another turn or two, we're in front of a closed door. "Here you are."

"My own room?" I clarify. The edges of his lips twitch. Does my uncertainty amuse him? Of course it does. Just because he hasn't hurt me yet, and just because he made me a sandwich doesn't make him any less of an Ivanov.

"For now. Once the wedding takes place, you'll move into my room." He gestures with his chin at the door at the end of the hall. It faces the hall, as though holding power over the other rooms.

I reach for the door handle, but his hand wraps around mine, stopping me. Warmth skyrockets up my arm at his touch.

"Lena," he says, cupping my chin with his free hand and drawing my face toward him. "I know this isn't what you want but understand there is no way out of it. If you try to run away, if you try to wiggle free of this agreement, there will be trouble. Not just between our families, but between you and me."

"Trouble between you and me?" I narrow my eyes. "You arrogant prick."

His lips spread into an amused grin. "There's the fire I saw before." He pinches my chin harder. "I find it refreshing, but don't mistake that for tolerance. You'll be a good wife. An obedient wife, or you'll face the consequences."

He lets go of my chin and reaches behind me, patting my ass.

I shuffle away from him, comprehending what he means.

"My father may allow this marriage, but he will never forgive you abusing me." My voice shakes, but I'm not sure if it's from exhaustion of the day, the fear of his threat, or because there's an electric current running straight to my pussy from his meaning.

"I won't abuse you, Lena." He lets me go, pushes the bedroom door open, and flicks a light on for me. "But I will not tolerate disobedience from my wife. Children misbehave, and if that's how you behave, that's how you'll be treated." He brushes my hair away from my shoulders. "Now, off to bed, little Lena. I have calls to make."

He doesn't even wait for me to speak or to move, he simply walks off back down the hall toward the front foyer and disappears down another hallway. As straightforward as this place seemed at the beginning, I doubt I'd be able to find him easily now if I needed to.

"Bed, Lena!" His voice carries easily down the long corridor to me. I fist my hands; the urge to scream back at him pulls on me. But in the end, I barge into the room and slam the door behind me.

CHAPTER 8

icah

I've never been much of a believer in breakfast being the most important meal of the day. But today's different. Today, it's important for other reasons besides nutrition.

Lena's awake and pacing around the guest room I put her in last night, but she hasn't stepped one toe outside it. I turn off the surveillance footage on my phone and decide to hurry her along. If she thinks she can spend the rest of our lives together hiding, she has more than a little eye opening to do.

The door's locked when I try to open it. I have the key in my nightstand, but there's no need to show all the cards in my hand at one time. I lightly rap my knuckles on the door and wait.

"Lena." I press my hands against the door frame and stare at the door as though if I stare hard enough, I'll be able to make out her form on the other side. And it is a delectable form. I

KEPT BY HIM

may have been busy keeping up with the deal making last night, but I had plenty of opportunity to take in her generous curves. The woman would have earned my father an excruciatingly large profit on the market. She has no idea how lucky she is to have been given to me instead.

"Lena, open this door," I call. There's some shuffling, but nothing else. "If I have to break it down, there's going to be a problem. And you don't want a problem with me this early in the morning." Or any time of day, but she'll have to learn this the hard way. I'm not an easy man, and no matter her age, I will take her over my knee if she gives me trouble. She's mine now. Mine to play with and mine to punish.

The door yanks open and she's there, standing right in front of me with her hair a mess from sleeping, and her eyes narrowed on me.

"Is that how everything gets resolved with you? Violence?" She holds the door against her body. Does she really believe she can keep me out of the room?

"You haven't seen violence yet," I remind her.

She pinches her lips together and a cherry blush rises to her cheeks.

"I don't want this door locked again." I push off the door frame. "Do you understand me?"

"Why? Are you afraid I'll have big parties in here and you won't be invited?" Thick sarcasm drips from her words.

Men twice her size would think again before using such a tone with me. Obviously, she's been sheltered—spoiled.

I shove the door out of her hand and advance on her. Every step I take forward, she takes one backward until I have her pressed against the dresser on the opposite wall. Her hands fly back to steady herself but being trapped only seems to infuriate her more. Steam would rise from her body if it were possible.

"I'm not afraid of anything. This is my house, princess. And you'll follow my rules here. You are never to lock yourself behind a door. Ever." I lean forward, covering her hands with my own. The edge of the dresser has to be cutting into her palms, but she keeps a steady expression.

"Whatever. Fine." She pulls her hands out from beneath me, but I don't move. She's nicely caged, and I'm keeping her that way until we have a little talk.

"Yes, sir would be more appropriate, but we'll get to that later."

Anger flashes in her silver blue eyes, but something else happens, too. Her pupils expand, her lips part slightly. If I trail my fingertips along the soft skin of her throat, will she tremble out of arousal or from fear? Either will do, but my gut tells me she's already making her panties wet from our brief interaction.

"There's breakfast in the kitchen. You need to come eat."

"I'm not hungry." She has to lean away from me in order to raise her defiant chin, but she manages without bumping into me.

"I didn't ask if you were. I said you need to eat, and you will." I inhale the sweet smell of her shampoo. She's not as tall as me, not by any stretch of measurement. Her head comes up to just below my chin. I could tuck her in perfectly beneath me like a puzzle piece snugly in place.

A small part of me likes this idea, her fitting right into my body, folding her in place with me. Her tongue runs along her bottom lip and another part of me likes that even better. I move my position away enough, so she won't feel my cock getting hard for her. Women use seduction as a weapon. I'm not easily fooled by it, but I won't have her embarrassing us both by attempting to wield her sexuality against me.

"I don't have any clothes." She captures my gaze, not giving me an inch. What she doesn't give, I'll take.

"You're wearing clothes now." I slide my finger between the thin fabric of the strap and her shoulder, gliding along until I can feel the swell of her breast.

Instead of smacking my hand away, like I expect, she moves up to her toes and tries to level our glares. There's a fierce streak in her. It's a good sign. My father would crush her easily otherwise.

"It's not mine. And it's all I have here."

I let the strap snap back onto her shoulder and take a step back, leaning to my right and opening a drawer. There are clothes stashed inside.

"There are clothes here. And in the closet. I'm sure you'll find something that fits." I've yet to have a woman have to make her walk of shame in the nude. But Lena's not one of those women. There is no place for shame with her. She's to be my wife. She'll have the Ivanov name. Nothing but pride and confidence should touch her.

"They aren't mine. And I won't wear your whore's clothing." She turns her nose up, taking the opportunity to slide away from me and move to the window.

I shut the drawer and lean my hip against the dresser, folding my arms over my chest. How best to deal with this princess brat? She deserves a red ass, maybe some time with her nose pressed firmly into the corner to show her I won't tolerate disrespect.

But it's our first day together, and in all fairness—not a word typically associated with me—she's been through an ordeal at the hands of both my father and hers.

"I will have your things brought over this afternoon. Your clothing anyway. If there's any sort of sentimental stuff you want, you'll have to go over to your father's house and get it yourself. I won't waste my men's time by picking through your things."

"I don't want their dirty hands on my belongings." Her mouth scrunches up and for a moment, I think she's going to spit at me. But at the last second, she turns toward the window. The blinds are slanted enough to let in the morning sun, but not give a clear view of the city below.

"Well, princess brat, I'll see if your father will pack your panties himself personally. Just for you," I say to her back, enjoying the way her muscles tighten beneath her creamy skin. The back of the dress dips low, showing off her toned body.

"Don't call me that. I'm no princess and I'm not a brat." Her voice raises enough that I drop my hands and march to her.

I grab her face with one hand and push her head back until I'm glaring down at her. She slaps at my hand, but it won't do any good. Her nostrils flare, probably in frustration that I have her and won't let go.

"Never raise your voice to me. You will talk with respect when you address me. Am I clear?"

She stops smacking at my arms and drops her hands to her sides. It's the closest thing to an acceptance I'm going to get this morning. And time's running out. I have to get across town to a meeting. Being late isn't something anyone would comment on, but it's not something I tolerate even for myself.

"Good." I release her. A red marking of my fingers lingers on her cheeks. "Now. I have a meeting. Eat breakfast naked for all I care, but you will eat something. I'll be back around seven tonight. I expect you to be ready."

"For what?" She frowns; maybe she heard the tiny tremor in her voice as clearly as I did. Showing weakness pisses her off. We're the same in that regard, but the difference is she's allowed her weakness. She has me to hide behind, to lean on.

"For dinner."

"I need to dress special for dinner?" She tilts her head to the side, staring at me like she's trying to understand the meaning between my words.

"We're going to my restaurant. My family will be there, so dress appropriate and be on time." As I turn for the door, I notice the bed hasn't been slept in. The covers are all neatly in place, not so much as a wrinkle.

"I slept on the chaise," she tells me, catching my line of sight.

"Why?" Like everything else in my home, the bed is luxury. Sleeping on a cloud would be less comfortable than the bedding in this room.

"I fell asleep." She shrugs.

Niko's waiting for me; I don't have time for word games.

"Why didn't you fall asleep on the bed?" I slide my hands into my pockets and take a small step away from her, giving her some space to herself.

She glances away. I don't think she wants to talk about it, which makes me even more interested.

"I was just sitting there for a few minutes thinking, the next thing I knew it was morning." She blushes. As confessions go, this was about as incriminating as Mother Teresa snagging a biscuit for herself at the food line.

"What were you thinking about?"

She raises her eyes to mine and for the first time, I see the slight puffiness around them. The woman hasn't slept well in days, and I'm positive she's been crying recently. Why wouldn't she be, she'd been kidnapped and now is being forced to marry into the family that stole her from the street.

"Nothing important." She runs her hands up and down her arms.

"Nothing exciting either, I guess since it put you to sleep."

She rolls her eyes. A gesture that normally pisses me off, but she's reacting to my lame attempt at levity, so I let it go. She's going to have a hard enough day ahead of her.

"Did my father's men hurt you when they took you?" I ask her, sensing a dark cloud lurking off in the shadows.

She blinks then shakes her head. "No, not really. I mean the drug they used made me sick, but other than that, I wasn't hurt."

I know what drug she means. A cocktail my brother, Igor, concocted years ago. It eventually renders the victim unconscious, but first it messes with their mind, makes them dizzy, gives them a headache as strong as a migraine. Some people become nauseated. The effects sometimes take days to fade.

"Are you still feeling ill?" I should have asked her these questions yesterday.

"No. The headache was gone when I woke up, I just had a little upset stomach. But I'm fine now." She pads over to the chaise, her bare feet making no sound against the plush gray carpeting. When she sits down, the hem of the dress rises, exposing a dark purple bruise on the outside of her knee.

"What's this?" I move to her and point to the bruise. If those assholes touched her while she was unconscious, if my father gave the go-ahead to use her while she was in that holding cell in the stable, I'm not sure I'll be able to stop myself from bringing it to him.

She bends to see what I'm pointing at, then brushes my hand away. "It's nothing. I hit my knee on the bed frame back at the…" She lifts her eyes to mine. "The stable."

The weight of her disgust presses down on me. It's not a proud feature of my family. But it is my family. I won't speak out against them, not even to her.

My phone buzzes. I'm late.

I text Niko then stash the phone back in my pocket. "I have to get moving. There's breakfast in the kitchen, eat it. If you'd rather, I can have one of my men take you to your father's house and you can pack your things this afternoon."

The corner of her mouth twitches upward and for a second I think she's going to smile. But she recovers quickly, stashing her joy before it can fully form.

"That would be good, yes." She looks at the bed. "Thank you."

"Dimitri will be here at one o'clock to bring you to your father's. I want you to rest this morning. Pick out something from the closet just for today."

Her gaze hardens.

"You would rather show up at your father's house in the same dress you were wearing yesterday?" I point to the skirt. "It's all wrinkled."

Her jaw clenches tighter. I'm not making a case, and I don't need to. If I tell her to pick something, she should just fucking pick it.

"I won't have you giving your father any reason to think I'm mistreating you. There's peace today between our families, Lena. Do you really want to do anything that will mess that up?"

"Maybe you could have thought of that before your family kidnapped me and forced me here," she snaps.

"It's not that simple, and you know it." My phone dings again. "I'm not arguing with you, I'm telling you. Don't wear that to your father's this afternoon. Pick something else; you can burn it later if you want." I'm not sure what makes me offer that suggestion, but it seems to do the trick.

"You should go. You're late," she says and walks to the en-suite bathroom, closing the door gently. I wait for a soft click to signal she's locked the door, but nothing comes. Satisfied that she will at least be able to behave herself while I'm gone, I grab my phone and shoot off a message that I'm on my way.

Once in the elevator, I send off orders to my men. We all have our duties for the day. Dimitri is the lucky bastard picked to babysit my fiancée for the afternoon.

Lucky bastard, indeed.

CHAPTER 9

*L*ena

I'm in the kitchen washing my breakfast dishes when a long chime rings. I turn off the water to listen, and again it rings. Leaving the pan in the sink, I make my way through the winding hallways to the main entrance just as the elevator doors slide open.

Micah said he wouldn't be back until tonight. Stupid elevator, I have no way to stop someone from entering when they aren't supposed to. I don't even have my phone to call for help.

A man steps off the elevator carrying four full bags. He's dressed similar to Micah with his dark suit and his black hair slicked back from his face.

"Lena?" He brings his gaze to meet mine.

I squeeze my hands together. "Who are you?" I'm a third of his size; even if I ran at him to knock him off balance, I'd probably only end up bouncing onto my ass.

"Dimitri, Micah's cousin," he says with a nod and walks to the table between us. Pushing aside the vase he puts the bags down. "Micah said to bring you these." He reaches behind him and pulls out a cell phone. "And give you this."

I stare at him for a long moment, before I take it from him. It's mine, and it's fully charged.

"He said whatever doesn't fit, put to the side and he'll take care of it later." He pushes the bags toward me.

"You went shopping?" I ask him, while digging into the bags. I pull out a t-shirt, a dress, a pair of jeans—all the right size.

Dimitri snorts. "No. I don't... shop. I picked them up from the stores I was told to."

"Micah said I was going to my father's house this afternoon to get my own things."

Dimitri frowns. "That won't be possible today. Things came up. He wanted you to have your phone in case you need him, his number's already programmed in." He points to my hands cradling my lifeline to the real world. "And here's the house code. For an emergency only." He pulls a folded-up piece of paper from his jacket and hands it to me.

"What came up?"

He shrugs. "Things. He'll be home late tonight."

"Late?" Am I really supposed to just sit here alone waiting for him to come home like some lost puppy waiting for her master? "What about dinner?"

"Like I said, things came up." He puts his hands up like he wants nothing to do with this discussion.

"I'll find my own way to my father's house then. I don't need you to take me. I'm sure my brother can pick me up."

"Micah said you're to stay here. He doesn't want you leaving today."

"What am I supposed to do, just sit here and stare at the walls?"

"I don't know, I gotta go. My suggestion, stay out of trouble." His eyes soften a bit, like he's a big brother warning his little sister. "The Ivanovs aren't a family to fuck with. You're lucky to be marrying Micah. Roman could have done much worse to you."

"So lucky." I grab the bags from the table. "Thank you, Dimitri, for bringing these."

The elevator arrives and he steps inside. When he looks back at me there's a touch of warning in his expression. "Look. Make the best of it, right?" This is his best try at advice.

"Yeah. Make the best."

Once he's gone, I take the bags to my room and dump them onto the bed. There's at least two weeks' worth of clothing here, including three dresses. They aren't my things, but at least they aren't from the closet of misfit one-night stands either. Everything he has in the dresser and the closet is brand new, tags are still on everything, but I'm not ignorant about what they really are. Who they were really for.

Dimitri wasn't at Roman's house last night, so he couldn't realize I was wearing the same dress.

I shove the clothes in the closet to one side then go about hanging the things Micah has bought for me. As a young girl I fantasized about my knight in shining armor being so sweet as to go shopping for me. To bring me a beautiful ball gown to wear with him when we met the king. After I finish clearing a drawer in the dresser and filling it with my new things, I stare down at the panties. Black lace and satin undergarments. Did Micah request these or did the sales lady already know his preferences?

Once everything's put away, and I've folded the paper shopping bags and stashed them behind the dresser, I change into a pair of jeans and t-shirt. I find a pair of sandals among the shoes and slip them on. I run a quick finger comb through my hair, working out the tangles and head back into the kitchen to finish cleaning up.

* * *

Skyscrapers block the sun, casting a pinkish orange shadow around the buildings as it begins to climb down from its daily perch. I lean my forehead against the window, staring at the city before me from the window seat in my bedroom. There's an entire apartment outside my door, but I haven't set foot in any of it.

This isn't my home.

I can't deny how beautiful it is, but it's not mine. I don't belong here. Sighing, my breath creates a circle of condensation on the window and I swipe my fingertip through it. This can't be the rest of my life, tucked away waiting for my husband to come home and let me out.

My father warned me about this. He tried to tell me how things were going to be for me, but I refused to listen. I wouldn't accept that my position in the family was to be used like this.

You cook, you take care of the household, you be there for your husband, that's what you do.

His words come back to me now and the same anger rolls into my chest. I'm more than that. I can do more than make a pot of coffee and spread my legs when he commands it.

As if on cue, my phone pings from the dresser. I'd left messages with Marie and Tanya that I was alive but didn't go into details of what all had happened. Unraveling my legs from beneath me on the window seat, I get my phone.

Let's parteeee

Nine o'clock Katfish

Tanya's obsession with my brothers' new club doesn't seem to be fading in the same timeframe of her other obsessions. I start to text her that I can't make it, but my thumbs freeze.

Why can't I make it?

Micah isn't home to stop me, and he gave me the elevator passcode.

Instead of texting her back, I hit the call button to get her on the line.

"Lena! Thank God you answered. I was worried," Tanya yells through the phone. Music thumps behind her.

"You're already at Katfish?" I ask, stalking to the closet.

"No, Marie and I are at Kristian's, we're heading to the club next. You'll come, right? Your dad doesn't have you locked up?"

My father?

"Tanya, I'm not at my house. My father—" I stop. She doesn't know, no one knows, I can still have a night of freedom before the word spreads through the families and I'm roped down.

"You headed to the club now?" I flip through the dresses in the closet. The three Micah had sent over are good for dinners, but not clubbing. I need something more erotic. I'll have to wear something from the whore selection.

"Yeah, you're coming, right?"

I pluck a black slip dress from the rack. Close enough to my size to make it work.

"On my way."

CHAPTER 10

ena

The bouncer standing outside Katfish greets me with a warm smile and waves me inside. I've only met him once, and his name escapes me, but I thank him and head inside.

"Lena!" Someone grabs my arm and yanks me from the main entrance into the coat check hallway.

I pull free of the grasp, ready to fight, until I recognize him. Jakub, my older brother.

"What are you doing here?" he asks, glancing behind me. "Is *he* with you?"

"Hi, Jakub. I'm fine, thanks. No harm done while I was being kept in a fucking cell of the fucking Ivanov family, Jakub. You shouldn't be so concerned; you'll worry yourself into a stomach ulcer!" I shove at his shoulders.

Dominik is the oldest and has always been the fierce protector of our family. But Jakub doesn't have the same worries the oldest son has; he spent more time with me growing up. He knows me better than my father, better than Dominik.

He grabs my hands and holds them in front of me, staring at me with sad eyes and a fierce frown. He's torn.

"I am concerned, Lena." He pulls me further down the hall, away from prying ears. "Are you okay?" He looks me over, checking for some sign of abuse. As though anything done on the inside isn't as bad as what could have been done to the outside.

"I'm fine." I tug my hands away from him and brush my hair from my eyes. "I'm okay. I promise. Other than being thrown in my trunk and drugged, no one's done anything to me."

His jaw tightens. "What are you doing here? Dominik said we weren't able to contact you until the wedding."

Of course. Keeping me isolated is probably their way of trying to keep me in control.

"I'm meeting Tanya and Marie. Have you seen them?" If I can keep my confidence up front, maybe it will shield how much I'm shaking on the inside. I've defied Micah Ivanov. When he gets home and finds me gone, he's going to have to react.

"You shouldn't be here." Jakub frowns.

"Jakub. I have the rest of my life to be annoyed by the Ivanov family. Give me tonight. After what happened, let me have a little freedom."

He sighs and tilts his head up to stare at the ceiling. When he was younger, he told me he did this to ask our mother for guidance on how to deal with me. I think that was just his way to guilt me into behaving.

"Fine. But no trouble, Lena. I'm serious. You stay for a few drinks, then you go back." He checks his watch. "I'll have a car ready for you in one hour. Not a second more. Understood?" He tries to give me his stern brother look, but he's never quite mastered it the way Dominik has.

"Of course." I smile and bat my lashes at him. He only shakes his head, knowing full well I'll do what I want, and he won't be able to stop me.

"One hour, and if you don't get in the car on your own, I'll call Dominik, or worse, Micah."

Moving up to my toes, I press a chaste kiss to his cheek. "Tattletale." I laugh.

"Have fun while it lasts, little sister," he says and gestures toward the main room with his chin. "I saw Tanya at the bar a few minutes ago. But I think they have a VIP section on the first floor."

"Thanks." I hug him tight then hurry off through the crowds to find my friends.

Tanya finds me first. With wineglasses in both hands, she rushes up to me and hugs me, spilling some white wine on my arm.

"Hey, you made it!" she yells in my ear over the booming music. "Fuck, Lena, this dress!" Her eyes go wide when she pulls back and looks at the painted-on dress I'm wearing. The neckline dips deep between my breasts, down to my belly button. I have never been so thankful for the belly bootcamp class I tortured myself with while in Poland. The only purpose had been to get away from my father's men and his nagging, but it worked to my advantage.

"Tanya, look, I have to talk to you. Something's happened." I take a glass from her and hook my arm through hers. "But I only want to go through it once, so let's get to the table with Marie and I'll tell you both."

She knits her brows together. "It's something bad."

I pull her along toward the VIP section. "It's not something great, but it could be worse."

"It has to do with whatever happened after you left the café the other day. Your father was so mad, and Dominik, I thought he was going to burst a blood vessel when we told him you left hours ago."

Once we're at the far corner table and I've given Marie a hug and assured her I'm fine, we sit down. There are dampeners set up on the outline of the section, so we can still hear the music, but it doesn't drown out our conversation.

"I love this place now that Jakub's done his magic. Your brothers are going to blow the city away." Marie sips whatever fruity concoction is in her glass.

"I was hoping they'd change the name though," Tanya remarks.

I sigh and take a long sip of my wine. I couldn't care less what my brothers call their club.

"So, what did you want to tell us?" Tanya scoots to the same side of the table as Marie and gives me her undivided attention.

I finish the wine.

It's not strong enough.

"I'm engaged." I blurt out and reach over the table, taking Tanya's wine.

"What?" Marie's jaw slacks. "To who?"

"That's the thing. After I left the other day, there was some, well, my father arranged…"

"Spit it out." Tanya pats my hand. "We can put the pieces together on our own. Who did your father sell you off to?" Tanya's father has worked with mine in the past, so she understands my family better than Marie.

"Micah Ivanov." I say, then drown his name with the entire glass of Pinot Grigio.

"The Russian guy?" Tanya's eyes widen. I might as well have told her I was marrying the Pope.

"You mean, the tall one with black hair, and wears a suit all the time?" Marie asks.

I roll my eyes. Dominik always wears a suit, too. That doesn't really help specify a man in my life.

"He's got a scar along his jaw, and he looks really pissed when he sees you?" Marie's gaze isn't on me. It's drifted over my shoulder and a trail of ice runs down my spine.

He couldn't have found me so quickly.

Not so easily.

No. Not yet.

"Lena." My name drops behind me and I know it's from his lips. A warm hand lands on my shoulder, gripping me hard.

I close my eyes. It's stupid and childish, but maybe if I can't see him, he'll go away.

"Ladies." He greets my friends. "I'm sorry to pull Lena away, but it's time for her to come home."

"Come home?" Tanya asks, frowning at me. "You live with him now?"

"A lot has happened." It's pathetic, and my only answer.

Tanya just nods in response. Apparently having a high-level member of the Bratva standing over the table is enough to silence her.

"I'm not quite ready to go yet, Micah." I fold my hands together on the table, resolving to stay put.

His warm breath tickles my ear. "Don't make me carry you, Lena. You're in enough trouble, princess brat."

I bite the inside of my cheek. We're in public and to scream at him here would cause a scene that would embarrass my entire family. And provoke the Ivanov family.

"I'll call you guys tomorrow." I jerk my shoulder away from his grasp and stand from my chair. Both of my friends stare at me like I'm being led to my execution and they're helpless to stop it.

"Lena, be careful," Tanya yells at me when I turn away from the table.

A quick glance up at his expression, and I can see why she would say such a thing. He looks ready to kill. Another shiver runs over me.

"Let's go." He cups my elbow. To anyone looking at us, we appear to be just another couple making our way through the crowd. But he's gripping me hard enough that I wouldn't be able to yank free no matter how hard I tried.

As we walk past the coat check, Jakub steps out. I don't stop my stride. The last thing I need is to bring him into this mess. One Staszek in trouble with the Ivanovs is enough.

Once outside, Micah walks me to the SUV idling in front of the club. He didn't have the car parked. Just hopped out and went inside to grab his wayward fiancée.

Everyone's eyes are on me as I walk past the people waiting to get into Katfish. My skin burns from their curiosity, from their judgement.

Micah opens the back door of the SUV for me and helps me climb inside. I expect him to go up front like he did last night, but he's not being as generous. He slides in right next to me and slams the door shut.

"Home," he barks to the driver.

"Micah—"

"Not a word." He puts a hand up between us, and I swallow the rest of my words.

His man is driving us home. We'll talk once we're back at the apartment. When we're alone he'll listen.

Only I'm pretty sure I'm lying to myself.

* * *

Lena

. . .

It takes almost no time to get us back to Micah's place. Or maybe it's just the sensation of time flying for the condemned. Micah hasn't glanced in my direction since he slammed the door at the club. He's pissed, I get it, but such dramatics aren't necessary.

The ride up the elevator with Micah standing directly behind me, glaring at the back of my head, sets my nerves dancing again. With as much concealment as I can manage, I take calming breaths to slow my racing heart, to get my lungs to work in correct order. I won't lose against him; I can handle this and anything else the Ivanov family sends my way.

I step off the elevator as soon as the doors open enough for me to slither through and head directly toward my room.

"Lena." His heavy tone stops me. "Follow me." He saunters past me and continues walking straight down the main hallway toward the double doors leading to his room. Although I was tempted to explore, I hadn't bothered looking around today. Who knows what lurks behind the two mahogany doors.

"Now," he calls when he's halfway to his destination and I still haven't moved.

"Can't we talk here?" I hurry my steps and catch up with him quickly.

"We aren't going to be doing much talking."

Nothing about his declaration gives me a warm fuzzy feeling. My feet agree and cement themselves to the floor. I'm easily within his grasp, but I'm not moving.

"Lena." My name comes out on a heavy sigh. "I think you've been disobedient enough for one day, don't you?" He pulls open one door and gestures for me to get inside.

From my standpoint, I can see a seating area. A couch, a recliner. Nothing too ominous, but I'm not really in the mood for risks.

"What are you going to do?"

His dark eyebrows shoot up. "I told you if you disobeyed there would be consequences."

I swallow back the little squeak my nerves let loose. "What exactly does that mean?" I grip my handbag with both hands in front of me, as though in some dimension the five-inch pouch could ward off an angry Micah.

He cocks his head to the side, narrowing his eyes on me. I'm pressing the line with my questions, with my hesitation, but I can't seem to stop myself. A freight train would have an easier time of slamming to stop at this point.

"You were told to stay home today." He reminds me of my crime, but it doesn't answer my question. "Weren't you? Dimitri said he gave you the message. You have your phone, so I know he's not lying."

I press my bag, where my phone is safely tucked away, to my stomach. "How do you know I have my phone?"

His lips ease into a confident grin. "How do you think I found you so quickly, princess?"

Of course. He gave me the phone back so quickly because he put a tracker on it. As soon as I stepped foot out of the apartment, he was probably alerted.

"I understand you're not happy that I left. But you were supposed to be home. You said I would get to go to my father's house today. You said you were taking me out to dinner tonight." I hold his gaze, but it takes so much energy not to tear my sight away from him. Even with that damn grin plastered on his lips, I can see the frustration in him. He's not going to let this go.

"Things changed and you were made aware of that." He shakes his head. "It doesn't really matter, does it, princess? I told you to stay put, and you didn't. It's a fairly easy concept to understand—obedience."

My stomach knots and twists. I've heard this tone before. Dominik uses the same one when he's past the point of discussion. When he's already decreed the punishment for the crime in his mind and all that's left is to administer it.

"What do you want, an apology?" I raise my chin a fraction and straighten my spine. I am not a child and I will not be talked down to as though I am. "I'm sorry that I didn't sit around here and pine for your return, oh master and lord of the castle." I sweep my arm down in front of me while dipping into a curtsey. When I get back to my feet, his arrogant smile is gone. The devil is riding my way, and instead of locking the door, I opened it.

"You'll be saying *I'm sorry* soon enough," he promises and walks into the room. He shakes off his suit jacket, lays it over the arm of the recliner, and stands in front of the couch, beckoning me with a crooked finger. "Now, Lena. I had to leave a very important meeting to go find you. I'm not going to wait all night."

My bedroom is only a few hundred feet behind me. I might be able to outrun him, even in my heels. But he has the key, and he already told me not to lock the door. How much do I want to risk going against him once more today?

With my head held high, my shoulders rolled back, I walk straight into the room. I toss my purse onto the recliner and fold my arms, ready to listen to whatever lecture he's concocted. He'll probably take away my phone, and he won't let me go to my father's, that's for certain. Whatever else he throws at me, I'll handle gracefully.

"Take off your shoes." He flicks his hand toward the red stilettos I found in the closet of misfit mistresses. They aren't exactly my size and have left my toes squished all night. Getting out of them is a luxury. While keeping my eyes locked on his—a feat I wasn't sure I had the energy to conquer—I kick the shoes off. Instant relief floods my poor toes.

His eyes travel down my body, surveying the dress, and then my feet. He gives a victorious grin.

"Guess the clothes came in handy, huh?" He points to my reddened toes. "You'll be swollen tomorrow. You shouldn't have worn them if they hurt like that."

"If you want to discuss my wardrobe, we can do it in the morning. I'm tired." I force a bored sigh.

His left eyebrow arches and he begins to unbutton his sleeve. "You aren't going to bed yet, princess."

My skin crawls every time he calls me that damn nickname. I never asked to be the youngest in my family, or the only girl. I never wanted all the attention that was sprayed in my direction.

With his dark eyes settled directly on me, he rolls up one sleeve and then the other to his elbow. It shouldn't bring any level of excitement to me, but heat spreads from my pussy upward to my belly. It's because of his sculpted body. No matter his level of asshole-ness, the man is attractive. It's a nonconsensual response.

"Take off your panties." He sits on the couch and places his hands on his knees. "Then pull up your skirt."

My ass cheeks clench at the indication he's making.

"I'm not going to let you hit me," I say, taking a wide step back.

He pats his right thigh. "You're right. You aren't going to let me do anything. You're going drape yourself over my knee and then you're going to *ask* me to give you the punishment you deserve."

A jolt of electricity erases all thought from my brain.

"Why would I do that?" I finally pluck the right words from the windstorm my brain has become.

"Because if you don't, I'll save your punishment for when my men arrive in thirty minutes. You interrupted my meeting, so they are coming over here tonight to finish it. I'm sure they wouldn't mind watching your ass turned red for the trouble your little trip caused them."

The image he describes forms in my mind. I have no doubt he'd do such a thing, adding humiliation to my pain. They'd laugh at me—at the Staszek bitch getting what's coming to her.

"What's it going to be, Lena?" Micah runs his right hand up and down his knee, like he's warming it for me. As though my entire body isn't already on fire from embarrassment.

I haven't been spanked since I was a small child, and it wasn't even a spanking but a smack to my butt after my mom caught me stealing the bag of cookies in the pantry.

"I—Micah, I'm sorry. It's been a really hard week."

Understanding edges its way into his hard glare. "None of that was your fault. But tonight was all you. Now let's get this done. Over my knee and ask for your punishment."

I have only one hope left. Once I'm in position, he'll let me back up with a warning that next time he'll go through with it. This could be a test. Just to get me to understand what he can make me do—what he can do to me.

Clinging to that notion, I shuffle myself to his side until my knees touch his.

"Your panties," he reminds me. "Remove them."

I raise my eyes up to the ceiling. How am I going to get through this? Inch by inch, I pull up the tight-fitting skirt of the ridiculous dress until I can snag the elastic of my panties. His attention slides down my body to my hands as I roll them over my hips and push them down to my feet. I bend over to pick them up, but he snags them before I touch them.

"I'll keep these." He puts them on the couch cushion beside him. An insult burns my tongue, but the heat spreading across my cheeks helps keep it inside my mouth.

"Over." He pats his leg again.

I raise my eyes from him, focusing instead on the arm of the couch as I bend over and crawl over his lap. He raises his right knee, tipping my head lower and my ass higher. I grab hold of a pillow and hug it to my chest, pressing my face into the couch.

Any second now, he'll let me up with a warning. I've learned my lesson well enough. We can finish this now.

"Skirt." He tugs on the hem of the dress.

"What?" I look back over my shoulder at him.

"The skirt of your dress—pull it up," he says again. There's no hint of reprieve in his dark eyes. Nothing but resolve.

Squeezing my eyes shut, I turn away from him and reach behind me.

"All the way up, Lena, to your waist," he instructs.

Gathering up the material in my fists, I drag it up until my bare ass is fully exposed to him. Tears build behind my eyes, but I hold them. I won't allow him to witness my mortification.

"There." He pats the low curve of my ass. "Now we're almost ready to start."

The last bit of his instructions comes to my mind. I'm supposed to ask him for this.

"Unless you'd rather wait until my men get here?" He sounds genuinely curious, but it's a front. All of this is just for show.

When I swallow, there's a lump in my throat. It's my pride, all balled up and ready to be swallowed down whole.

"Will you please—" I fist my hands into the pillow. I can't do it.

"They'll be here in probably twenty minutes," he says, running his hand over my ass in circles. If this were any other moment, and if he was any other man, it could be comforting, good even.

"Will you please punish me for my disobedience?" I let out a relieved sigh. Now he can let me up.

"Of course I will, Lena."

My eyes fly open just as the first crack of his hand hits my ass. Vibrations from the impact rush my body, but it's the shock that has me frozen.

The second smack to my rear jolts me back and the heat spreads over my cheeks.

Over and over again he peppers my ass with his open hand, not missing an inch. What starts as a blanket of warmth quickly ignites into an ember.

"Micah." I wiggle from side to side. "You made your point," I say, shoving my arm back between our bodies and trying to shield myself.

"No reaching back." He grabs my wrist and pins it to the small of my back. "And my point was made a while ago, this is your punishment. This is the consequence for bad girls who disobey."

The swats get harder and faster.

"Micah!" I wiggle more, but he only responds easily by maneuvering his leg from beneath me and trapping me between them. I can't get away, and he's got my wrist in such a death grip I can't get free that way either.

"Learn this lesson well, Lena, because if we have to repeat it, you'll be getting a taste of my belt," he promises as he increases the spanks once again. I smack the couch cushion in front of me and try to push out of the vise his legs have me in, but it's for naught. I'm only exhausting myself.

The tears I swore would stay behind closed lids spill down my cheeks.

"Please!" I beg as I try to throw my right hand behind me to stop the spanks if only for a moment. He captures that hand as well and now I have both hands pinned and my legs locked down. I'm completely helpless.

My ass is an inferno from his punishing hand, but he doesn't let up. Over and over again he spanks, moving his aim even a little lower to the tops of my thighs. But I'm out of fight, I'm out of pride.

I'm crying. Openly crying into the couch, while he continues to spank me like a disobedient brat. I should have stayed in; I should have found something else to do, maybe invited Tanya and Marie over here. Instead, I tried to show him what I thought of his authority.

And now he shows me what it really means.

"It's over, Lena," he says between my soft sobs. The couch muffles me enough that maybe I haven't completely embarrassed myself. The throb in my ass takes up all of my attention. How can I sit down now? I have to be black and blue and swollen.

Micah eases me up from between his legs and pulls me into his lap. I hiss as soon as the raw skin of my ass rubs against the smooth material of his trousers. He wraps his arms around my shoulders and pulls me into his chest, tucking my head beneath his chin.

I wipe the tears from my cheeks and take a slow breath in, hold for three seconds, and release.

"You did pretty good, Lena." His compliment surprises me and I push away from his chest to look into his eyes. If he's teasing me, I'll lose my temper. Where there was sternness before, there's warmth now.

"I don't ever want to do that again." My voice shakes, but it can't be helped.

He breaks into a smile. "Good, then maybe we won't have to." He tilts his head to the side. "Except for fun."

"Fun?" My brows furrow. "Why would that ever be fun for me?"

His arm wrapped around my torso tightens and his free hand pushes my legs apart. "Don't fight me now, unless you want to go back over my knee."

It's only curiosity that keeps me obedient as he slides his hand up my thigh to my sex. With a featherlike touch, he glides his finger through my folds, flicking my clit as he removes his touch and brings his finger up to my view. My juices have soaked him.

A new heat spreads across my cheeks, and a new sort of mortification takes over when he sucks his finger and licks off my arousal.

"I…" I have nothing to say.

"It's a good thing, Lena." He cups my cheek, pulling me to look him in the eye again. "Once we're married, it will be good between us. We'll make it work."

What is he talking about?

"You just had me over your lap and spanked me. You just… my butt hurts so much I'm not sure I'll be able to sit tomorrow."

He shrugs. "Maybe not. I wasn't as hard on you as I would have been if we knew each other more."

"More? We don't know each other at all!" I elbow away from him and get to my feet, quickly shoving my dress back down to cover myself. He's seen more than enough of my body tonight.

He rises to his feet with me, and hovers over me.

"I don't want this marriage, Micah. Neither do you." I lift my chin.

He reaches out and trails his fingertip down my cheek. "You cried so prettily."

My heart hammers with his words, not with what he said, but how aroused he sounds when he says it.

"I don't want to cry." It's a pathetic thing to say, but I'm not thinking clearly.

"You will. And it will be good. You'll see." He cups my cheek and leans in, the scent of his spiced aftershave envelops me just before his lips press against mine. His hand snakes behind my head, into my hair where he makes a fist.

It hurts, but the tenderness of his kiss washes it away. His tongue brushes against my lips, as though asking permission to enter. But all gentleness ends as soon as I give him entry. The kiss turns possessive and hard. My lips will be as swollen as my ass, but I can't seem to find the strength to shove him away. Or the desire.

My toes curl into the carpet as he presses his body against mine. Every bit of him is touching me. Every. Bit. His cock is hard, and he presses it firmly against my hip.

Only when he releases me do I remember to breathe. His brown eyes meet mine as he slowly lets go of my hair.

"It's been a long night for you. Wash up and get in bed."

I stare at his lips. How can a man with such power, such steel in his heart bring about such warmth and longing with a kiss?

"Lena. I'm going to have some boxes brought up tomorrow. I want that closet packed up and I never want to see you in one of those dresses again." He pinches my hip and smiles.

"Will you... I mean, is that the last time?" I look over at the couch, hoping he catches my meaning.

"From what I've heard about you, I doubt it." He wipes my cheek. "No more tears tonight, or I won't be able to wait until our wedding to take you to my bed."

I must look shocked by his words because he laughs. It's the first time I've heard it. It's earthy and genuine.

"Go to bed, Lena." He spins me around and pats my ass.

I start forward and go to pick up the shoes, but he stops me.

"Leave those. I'm going throw them away. They're too small for you."

My toes.

I look down and wiggle them. They don't hurt anymore, but I'll probably have a blister tomorrow.

"Good night, Micah," I say and hurry from the room.

Anger should be ruling my mood. I should be ready to throw things and demand to be taken home. I should pick up my phone and call my father and tell him Micah hit me. That I'm being abused.

Back in my room, I open the closet door to the full-length mirror. I pull up the dress and turn to look at my ass expecting to see black and blue markings.

But all I see are red splotches and one very distinct handprint. My fingers gently trace over the print, over Micah's hand.

This is a dangerous place to be. Micah is a dangerous man. And I'm not sure I have the weapons to fight him.

CHAPTER 11

Micah

My father's boisterous laugh warns me he's in my office before I reach the door. It's already been a shitstorm of a day, and now I have to deal with him. This restaurant isn't just a way to bring the family closer to legitimacy; it's the one thing in all of our dealings that's completely mine to run. No oversight, no one to answer to or run shit by first. It's just mine.

But my father forgets.

"Hey." Dimitri catches me as I reach for the door. "Give him a minute."

I drop my hand from the handle. "What's he doing?"

My cousin grins.

"Who is he doing?" I made it clear the restaurant staff was off limits. We're running a clean business here; we can't have sexual harassment suits happening.

"He's been here a while waiting for you," Dimitri explains with a shrug.

"I don't want him manhandling the staff." I push through the door into my office. My father turns to me, a wide-eyed smile frozen on his lips. One of the waitresses, Tammy, Tanya, something like that, is sitting on his lap, playing with his tie.

"Micah. You're here. Finally." My father pats the girl's hip. "Back to work."

She slides off his lap and throws a wink his way before shuffling toward the door. As she passes me, I grab her arm.

"I want a word later." She lowers her eyes and nods. If she thinks she's going to get anywhere in this restaurant by cozying up to my father, I'm going to set her straight. And if Roman overstepped this afternoon, I'm going to have to apologize on his behalf, while not apologizing for him.

Some days I wonder if I'm going to finally tip off the tightrope I walk.

"Dimitri." I stop him before he walks away. "I'm running late. Call Niko and tell him to go my apartment and pick up Lena and take her to her father's house. She's going to get some of her things. Whatever she can't fit into the SUV, have a few guys go over tomorrow to get."

"You got it." Dimitri pulls my office door closed, leaving me to deal with Roman on my own.

"Did we have a meeting set up?" I slide my hands into my pockets. He's sitting at my desk, but he's still the head of this family. So like it or not, I'm going to remain standing on this side for the time being.

"No." He leans back in my chair. "You had a meeting with Joseph Staszek this afternoon."

"I did. He wanted to talk about his daughter. It had nothing to do with the deal he made with you."

"And?" He leans forward, all attentive now that we're talking about the Staszek family.

"And he informed me that he was cutting Lena from his estate. She'll inherit nothing once the marriage takes place. The deals he made with you for territory and all that stays the same, but she'll get nothing, which means I'll get nothing when he passes."

"It's all going to the boys." Roman nods. "It's not unheard of. More traditional than most these days, but I suppose we can't fight him on it."

"He's choking her out because of us," I say plainly, not that he'll give a shit. Why would he, the territory lines have moved, and he's gotten what he wanted from this mess.

"She'll have our name, and you'll see that she's taken care of." He shoves out of my chair with a grunt. "Not too well, don't waste your money on that Polish trash."

I fist my hands in my pockets. Lena's not trash. I may not know her well yet, but from what I've seen she's anything but that. I tease her by calling her a princess, but it's not completely a joke. So far she's shown herself more regal than any actual royalty I've met.

Even after I tanned her ass last night, she didn't come at me in a wild rage or throw a tantrum. She accepted her punishment, kept herself together, and took every swat to her ass with a grace I'd forgotten a woman could possess. The last girl I dated with any sort of regularity hadn't lasted half a dozen swats before she lost her mind and started hitting at me and cussing me out. It wasn't worth the fight—I'd let her leave and never called her again.

"What brings you here?" I change the topic. "Is something wrong?"

He shakes his head. "No, no, not at all. In fact, things are good, Micah. Real good." He grins. "Now that we have the train depot at our full disposal, we can increase our transports. I've already discussed with our partners up in New York, and they say they can handle twice the load we move now." His Russian accent thickens the more excited he gets about this venture.

"Twice?" I control my surprise. "The traffic was supposed to slow, not increase. Between the two clubs on the south side and this restaurant we're making good profits. They give us an income stream that lets us focus on other things." My office is secure, but there's still cause for caution. Roman's hand having been up the waitress's skirt, for one.

"Yeah, of course, of course. These businesses help us hide. I understand. I do, Micah. But your brother built us a line of income that is never ending." He makes his way to me, planting his heavy hands on my shoulders. "Igor built the traffic line from the ground up. It's a solid business. No reason not to expand when it's right there for the taking." His eyes peer into me as his hands tighten around my shoulders.

"Igor did an amazing job, I know," I agree. Igor did many great things for our family, for my father; his legacy should be more than the trafficking of stolen women.

"He was a strong man. He had visions for this family, for all of us."

I've heard this lecture before. The great saint that was my brother.

"I have visions for this family, too." I line my gaze with his. As the second son, I walked in Igor's shadow—gladly—my entire life. But I'm not the second son anymore. I'm the only son.

He raises his eyebrow. "I know you do." He pats my cheek. "And they are good ideas. Legitimize where we can. It's a solid plan. One our lawyers I'm sure are thrilled to see coming to fruition. But the money isn't in breadsticks and dance clubs. It's where we've always made our best money. How do the Americans say… sex, drugs, and rock and roll? Well, maybe not so much the rock and roll, eh?" He laughs and pats my cheek again. I don't recall him every patting Igor's cheek like a little boy.

"Your brother was a smart man." He points at me. "He knew when to move forward and when to back off." His smile still clings to his lips, but there's a warning there, underlining the words. Don't push him.

"Doubling the traffic would put us in danger. The payroll would have to double along with it. They can only turn the other cheek for so much." I appeal to the bottom line. The law enforcement that we've been able to hook to protect us won't take breadcrumbs anymore if my father expands too quickly.

"Eh, we'll work it out. Even if we do double the security payroll, we'll still make more in the long run. This is a good thing, Micah. Be happy for us."

"It's good news." I nod along with him because it's what he wants. And Roman Ivanov won't leave until he gets what he wants.

"Excellent." He grabs his coat from the back of a chair. Even when it's sunny and humid outside, the man carries his coat with him. An old habit, I think, of when he used it to smuggle for his old boss.

"One more thing," he says as he stops at the door. "The wedding will be this Saturday at my house. I expect you and that girl to be there Friday night for a celebration dinner."

We'd already discussed the ceremony being held at his place, but the dinner Friday night is new.

"Of course." There's no reason to disagree.

"The Staszeks won't be there, but I'm gracious enough to allow them at the ceremony." He frowns.

"Do you need me to do anything—for the expansion?" I offer before he decides I'm against him. Disagreeing with him is one thing; openly disapproving is something altogether different, and more dangerous.

"No, not right now. The hunters will increase their catches next month. We might need some readjusting then." He opens the door. "I'll see you Friday."

I nod. "Yes. We'll be there."

With fucking bells on.

CHAPTER 12

ena

My bedroom at my father's house was more welcoming after I'd returned from Poland than it is today. Nothing in here has the sense of home. Even my bed feels off when I sit on it. I've only been gone a few days, and already my past drifts into the distance.

"Need any more boxes?" Niko brings in another box that he's taped up for me to fill and drops it next to the dresser.

"This should do it," I say, looking at the other four he's made for me.

He looks around at what I've already accomplished in the two hours we've been in my father's house. Six boxes sealed and ready for moving, and three suitcases. Shit, maybe Micah's right to call me a princess. I haven't even packed my out-of-season clothing yet.

My cheeks heat at the thought of Micah. He had already left the apartment this morning when I gathered up the courage to go to the kitchen. I was lucky to avoid the awkwardness. Or maybe he wouldn't think anything was out of the ordinary. Maybe he spanked all of his past girlfriends and it was just another evening by his standards.

But it wasn't for me.

"I'll bring the suitcases down to the car. I think we can fit probably three of the boxes, so just let me know which three you want today. The rest will have to be moved tomorrow."

I silently nod and turn back to my dresser, picking up my mother's music box. Tears sting my eyes as I open the lid and the soft melody plays. I wish I could remember more of her than just this song. It's been years since I saw her face clearly in my memory or remembered the smell of her perfume.

I'm packing up my entire life into boxes. My father isn't home; the housekeeper said he had a meeting or some nonsense. I have no one here, and no one where I'm going.

"Lena?" Dominik's voice carries from the hallway.

Quickly, I snap the box closed and wipe the lone tear from my cheek.

"Here," I call.

Dominik saunters into my room, taking one look at the boxes and a dark cloud covers his features.

"Dad's not here," I say and pack the music box away.

"I know. Micah told him to stay away, that's why I'm here."

I huff. "Micah tells our father to jump and he does?"

"I think he couldn't face you." Dominik maneuvers around the boxes to me, glancing down at the half-packed box.

"Why not? This is my duty, right? To marry into some family that will bring our family prosperity?" I drop my hands from the dresser. I don't want anything else from this room. It's all tainted with hopes and dreams of a stupid young girl. "Except that's not what this is, right? This is punishment for what your wife did." Anger bubbles in my chest. Looking at him brings the dormant rage to life. "But instead of you or her dealing with the consequences, it's me."

"Lena. We had no way of knowing that shipment belonged to them," he says for the millionth time, and still, it does nothing to assuage my anger.

"If you had known, you wouldn't have stopped her. You would have still done exactly as you did," I accuse him. His jaw tightens, but I'm not done. "It's because of you and that wife of yours that this happened. Why are you here? To be sure I honor the commitment you and our father made on my behalf? To be certain I don't run away and leave you to clean up your own mess?"

"If there was another way to resolve this I would." Dominik frowns. He's telling me the truth; he would sacrifice himself for me if he needed to, but that doesn't make the hurt any less.

"I don't want this, Dominik," I say softly.

"Micah is a good man," Dominik says. "Kasia didn't want to marry me either."

"Micah is an Ivanov. You've always told me the Russians weren't to be trusted."

Dominik takes a deep breath. "Since when do you listen to me?"

"I'm afraid," I confess, keeping my eyes down. I can't bear to see his disapproval.

"It will work out, Lena," he promises, but how can he know? "We all make sacrifices for the family. I married a Garska for the same reason you're marrying an Ivanov."

I raise my eyes to his. Deep down, I know he's right. He had no choice in his wife; our father decided that it would happen.

"I need to hurry up." I work the box closed. Dominik takes the packing tape from me and seals it for me.

"Dominik." Micah's dark voice wafts from the doorway. The air grows thick instantly when I look up at him. He's frowning.

"Micah." Dominik puts the packing tape on the dresser and steps to my side. "I came to check on my sister."

"I can see that." Micah surveys the boxes. "Is this everything?"

"Yes." I hold myself straight, but don't quite meet his gaze.

"I can bring her to your place," Dominik says. "I'll take a load of the boxes with me—save your men some time."

Micah's lips tug into a half smile, but even that much is forced.

"No need. We'll be taking the car Niko's already filled. He'll use mine to pack these." He waves at what's left of my life tucked away in cardboard boxes.

"My wife hasn't met Lena yet. I'd like her to come to dinner tomorrow night."

Micah grins. "Sorry, she's busy."

"I am not," I interject.

Irritation flashes in Micah's eyes. I'm not picking sides between these chest-pounding apes, but I will be the one who decides my social calendar.

"You are." There's no wiggle room in his tone.

"I won't have you keeping her from her family." Dominik steps toward Micah. Not only are they the same build and height, their stern expressions match. It's almost comical, the way they are throwing around their authority.

"She has a new family to get to know. And seeing as your father all but threw her out of your family today, I don't see the problem."

"What?" I take a step forward, maneuvering around the box. "What does he mean?" I tug on Dominik's arm. His jaw tenses, but he keeps his glare settled on Micah.

"Do you not want to tell her?" Micah gestures toward me.

"Roman Ivanov won't allow us to attend the rehearsal dinner. We are only to attend the wedding on Saturday," Dominick informs me as though reading me a headline.

"The wedding's on Saturday?" I blink a few times. "Wait. Why can't they be there on Friday?" I ask Micah. "And how does that mean my father has kicked me out of my family?"

Micah stares down Dominik for a long moment then heaves a sarcastic sigh. "Okay, I'll tell her." He turns his gaze on me, but as soon as his eyes meet mine, the joy he cradled a moment ago softens. Another long beat passes before he finally speaks. "Your father has written you out of his will. You'll inherit nothing."

Out of nowhere a wrecking ball blows through my chest, whisking away my air. After a moment turns into two, then three, I finally remember to suck in air.

"He's disowned me?" I turn my attention to Dominik. "You knew. That's why you came here."

"No. I came to see you. But yes, I knew what he was doing. He is not kicking you out of our family. You will always be a Staszek."

"Until she is an Ivanov. Once she takes my name, she'll be part of my family," Micah explains.

Dominik turns to me, effectively blocking me from seeing Micah.

"He's not disowning you, but he doesn't want anything going to the Ivanovs. It's not you, Lena." Dominik softens his tone, but it doesn't take away the sting.

I take a slow breath in through my mouth and push it out through my nose. It's not enough to squelch my rattled insides, but it keeps me from crying.

"No, nothing about this is about me."

"Lena—"

"We should go." Micah moves in; his presence pushes Dominik to step to the side in order to avoid a confrontation.

"Give me a minute with her," Dominik demands. But he doesn't have authority in my life anymore. The reins have been handed over to Micah.

"We need to go," Micah repeats, keeping his voice firm and his eyes on me. Am I supposed to choose? I want neither of them. I want to crawl under my covers until the monsters leave, but none of that is going to happen.

"I'm imagining the two of you fighting. Like a real fight. Fists and blood, all that stuff." I move my gaze to my brother then to my fiancé. "I honestly don't know who I'd root for, or if I would just be happy you were both hurting."

Dominik's lips pinch together. Whatever he wants to say, he's going to keep it to himself.

Micah grabs hold of my hand. "That's enough, let's go." He tugs me along, and like the little pawn I am, I move from one room to the next and out of the house until I'm stored away in the passenger seat of the SUV.

As Micah pulls away from the curb, I look up at my bedroom window. Dominik stands there, his hands in fists. I can almost see the anger rolling off him.

"Where are we going?" I ask, turning away from my childhood home.

"Where do you want to go?" Micah's question surprises me.

"You sounded like we had to be somewhere."

"Your brother was upsetting you," he says.

"I was fine."

He glances over at me. "You were doing that breathing thing you do. You weren't fine."

"What?"

"When you get worked up, you do a breathing technique." He turns the car down a side street. "I dated a psychologist once. She used it for anxiety stuff. Is that what you have?"

"Let's just get this stuff home. I'd like to get my clothes unpacked tonight."

"I won't have my wife keeping secrets from me."

I look out the window, at the houses of old friends passing. Stores I used to sneak to with my allowance and buy candy before dinner. It all slips past me as I'm driven further and further away from where I started, from where I belonged.

"Then it's a good thing I'm not your wife yet." I lean back against the headrest and close my eyes.

He says something to himself, under his breath in Russian. I don't completely understand it, but I'm pretty sure he was cursing.

I turn toward the window, eyes closed and a smile tugging at my lips.

CHAPTER 13

M*icah*

I'm an asshole. It's just a fact, and I've never denied it. But when Lena's body sagged in reaction to finding out about her father's actions, I felt it in my soul. Branding *Asshole* right across my deepest self.

Nothing happening now is her doing. Everything is because of the actions of other people, but here she is taking the brunt of the punishment. She's angry, it vibrates off of her, but she's holding herself together, either to show me her strength or because she doesn't think she's safe enough to unravel.

I've done my homework and Lena Staszek has reason to hold her chin high when she walks into a room. And it has nothing to do with her father's station in his family, although to the outsider it seems that way. This woman of mine has more to her than she lets anyone see, more than I think her father knows about. I wasn't just bullshitting her when I said I won't have secrets. But after witnessing a few stones crumble from her exterior this afternoon, I'm willing to give her more time.

"The stuff from the closet is boxed up, can you help me bring it out here for the guys?" Lena asks while heading to her room once we're home.

"Lena, wait."

She pauses at the door, her hand already poised over the handle.

"Your things will be moved into my room." I announce my decision even as I'm making it.

She drops her hand and turns to me; shocked eyes line up with mine. "What? Why?"

"We'll be married in a few days and your things will have to be moved then anyway. Why bother unpacking only to repeat the process." I shrug off the decision as practical, but the truth, if I'm brave enough to admit it to at least myself, is I want her in my room. In my bed.

"I don't think we need to share a room." She gestures to the open spacing of our home. "There's plenty of space here for both of us. Once we say the vows, we can avoid each other as much as we want."

There's a shimmer of hope in her eyes even as the moments tick by with my silence.

"You don't really believe that do you, Lena?" I move to her side in case she decides she wants to bolt into her room. I've told her never to lock the door against me, but she hasn't proven to be the most obedient girl so far. A fact I'm not at all surprised or saddened by.

"Married couples live separate lives all the time." She keeps up the pretense, but the truth fades the light in her eyes. She knows it's an empty attempt.

But she's not wrong either. It's not as if my father and mother lived one life. My father and his many girlfriends had a life of parties and luxury while my mother stayed home with Igor and me playing the doting wife. She had her own circle of friends, wives of my father's associates but it wasn't the same life as my father's.

"We aren't going to be that sort of couple," I say.

Her eyes narrow as though she's trying to see past my clothing and into my heart. "What is it you really want, Micah? You're being forced into this just as much as me, so why won't you take the easy road here. I'll stay here, you stay there." She points at the double doors leading to my rooms. "And we'll say hi at the breakfast table now and then."

"And children?"

She blinks. Evidently, she hadn't figured them into her little equation.

"I'll need a son, preferably two, and I wouldn't mind a daughter."

Her cheeks burst into a blush, but I won't pretend I've triggered her sensibilities. It's a fresh bout of anger that's bringing the life to her cheeks. And she's gorgeous for it.

"A daughter so you can use her as a pawn, like me? Like my brother's wife was used?"

When I lean toward her, she presses her hands against my chest.

"Children, Lena," I whisper into her ear. Her breath catches, and she turns her face away. "You'll give me children, and to do that you'll need to be in my bed."

"I don't need to stay in your room for that to happen."

I laugh. "Are you always so practical?"

"When it serves my purpose, yes."

"I'm the same." I cradle her face in my hand and caress her cheekbone with my thumb. "And it serves my purpose for you to be in my bed, every night from now on."

"But we aren't married."

"You know as well as I do that the ceremony is a formality at this point. You're mine, Lena. Our families know it, the other families know it. It seems the only person who hasn't accepted it yet is you. But by the end of the night, you will too."

Her pretty pink lips part but she says nothing. She doesn't need to; her pupils have pushed all of her silver blue irises out of the way.

The elevator doors chime then slide open from down the hall.

"Boss, where do you want these?" one of my men calls to me. Three boxes are stacked on a rolling cart and he's bringing them toward us.

I bring my gaze back to hers.

"My room. All of them."

* * *

I've left Lena in my room unpacking her clothing. The closet in my room is the size of a small bedroom. She'll have plenty of space. Once she saw the closet and the bathroom, she didn't have much more fight in her about where she'd be spending her nights.

If only my father would budge so easily from his hopeless ambitions.

Niko paces my office. "I've never seen him so obsessed," he says, marching straight for the liquor.

"You had a nice chat with him then?" Any conversation with my father these days would make anyone take a nosedive into a bottle. But Niko handles him better than most. He worked close with Igor and now that he's my right-hand man, my father trusts him, respects him.

"Double the girls? Why would he put us in jeopardy like that? It's not that easy to turn the other way with fifty to sixty women being carted off through the train yard. Security is going to double; more hands will need to be greased."

Everything he says, I agree with, and he knows it. "I had hoped when he saw the profits from the legitimate businesses, he'd be open to phasing out the girls altogether and sticking to the drug line for extra revenue streams. The coke makes him more money than the girls, with less risk, less overhead. But he's got it in his head he can expand what Igor created."

Niko scoffs then downs a finger of vodka.

"What?" I ask, catching the little shake of his head. "What do you know that you aren't telling me?"

He pours another drink, downs it. After a long pause he turns a serious stare on me. "Igor hated that fucking train," Niko says flatly. "Hated it."

"What?" I press him. Niko was closer to my brother than anyone in our family. Igor didn't like the business approach I took. Roman coached him well while we were growing up on how to be the head of a family. Our family. It was never lost on me that I was the backup. It's the only reason I was allowed to get a full education. I was never meant to be the one in power. But Niko worked by Igor's side. He knew us both well growing up, but his work demanded that he stick by Igor.

Niko studies me as though assessing the risk of saying what's on his mind.

"Before the accident, Igor told me he was going to talk to Roman about closing the stables and expanding the drug line."

Igor never mentioned it to me, but I wasn't working the business as hard as Niko and him. I oversaw a small crew and focused on my business studies. The backup son has more freedom to pursue other avenues than being the heir. That is until the backup becomes the primary.

"Did he have the conversation?"

Niko finishes his drink. "I don't know. I didn't talk to him after that. A few days later is when he had the accident."

An accident that involved him and a traffic light. Igor held his liquor like it was just part of his bloodstream, but that night he'd been out of it. Not fit to drive, the bartender had said. Igor wouldn't be talked into handing over his keys but did promise not to drive home. He didn't make it two blocks before he wrapped his car and himself around the pole.

"Roman never said anything." I close my eyes and pinch the bridge of my nose. Even if Igor did have that sit down, Roman wouldn't have gone along with it. But Igor would have pushed harder; he would have stood up for what he wanted.

"It's been two years now. Maybe you can talk with him. You've proven yourself. He trusts you."

Igor was larger than life to my father; his death only made the shadow that much larger for me to get lost in. Roman trusts me, yes, but have I proven to him that I can lead this family into the next phase of prosperity?

Nothing indicates that's true.

"I tried to warn him about this expansion, but he won't listen." I get up from my chair and shake out of my jacket. "I'll try again after the wedding. Once this whole Staszek mess is behind us, maybe he'll be more clear-minded."

"Let's hope." Niko puts his empty glass on the bar. "I need to get over there. The doctor is coming tonight to check out the girls in the stables."

"You know, you don't have to do that anymore. Roman has his own men to do that. I'm sure Dimitri would be happy to take it over."

Niko pauses a beat. "Yeah, but I don't mind. Besides there's two new girls being brought in."

What does that have to do with anything? We have men for the small jobs and watching over the doctor while he checks over the girls is one of them.

"I'll see you tomorrow at the restaurant?" Niko says as he heads for the door.

"Yeah. I'm planning to be there all afternoon. The accountant is coming, and I want to meet with a broker about another location."

"You're expanding already?"

"Maybe. I want to see what the numbers are first. The sooner I get the restaurant booming, the easier it will be to get Roman's mind off the girls."

"I'm not sure steak and potatoes is going to bring as much profits as those girls but keep trying." Niko winks and leaves, closing the door behind him.

I sink into my office chair and power up my computer, ready to dive into more numbers. My email loads first and the top subject line erases my interest in work.

Subject: Lena Staszek School Transcripts & misc.

One click, and I jump headfirst down a rabbit hole.

CHAPTER 14

Micah

Lena's in the bathroom when I enter the bedroom. Looking around, I find little droplets of her influence. A laptop on the nightstand, a pair of slippers next to the bed. She wants the right side of the bed apparently. Her phone is charging on the dresser. The empty boxes are piled up in the sitting room that separates the bedroom from the small library. One of the things that drew me to this apartment was the master suite. If I moved my office to the library, I'd never have to leave the suite.

A textbook catches my eye. It's sitting on the dresser, next to her phone.

Discovering Psychology.

After reading over the information I received, the textbook doesn't surprise me. That she's left it out does, however.

"What are you looking at?" Her voice carries across the room.

I snap the book closed and show her the face of it. "Some light reading before bed?" I ask, enjoying how the color runs from her cheeks and her eyes widen. She's wearing a robe and her hair is tied up in a towel on top of her head. Her skin shines from whatever scrub she used, something with a heavy lilac scent from what I can tell. The makeup, what little she wears, has been washed away.

My cock wakes up to the sight of her purity. It's not because she looks virginal—I have no use for a woman who needs her hand held in bed—it's the natural beauty she possesses. The confidence rolling off of her as she stands in her robe, glaring at me from the bathroom door.

"It's just a book." She tries to sound casual, but her gaze fixates on the textbook in my hand.

"Try again," I prompt.

"What?"

"That was a horrible lie, try again. Go on, I'll give you another try. If you can come up with something convincing, I'll let the lies go. But if you can't do any better, then you'll have to accept a consequence." The memory of her bare ass draped over my knee pops into my mind, and my dick twitches against the zipper of my pants.

She worries on her bottom lip. It's alluring to watch her mind working. Since I already know the truth, nothing she says will work.

After a long pause she sighs. "It's just a book I've been looking at. It's nothing." To appear, I assume, like she couldn't care less if I believe her, she turns away from me and works the towel off her head, letting the long, wet tresses of her hair fall over her shoulders.

"You didn't even try that time." I thumb through the book then latch onto her glare again. "It makes me think maybe you like the consequences for being bad." I level an even stare on her. Her delicate throat works as she swallows hard and I imagine what it would look like to have my hand wrapped around it.

"You're imagining things." She snatches the book from my hand and moves to the dresser, opening the top drawer and shoving it inside. When she turns back toward me, her ass presses against the drawer and she folds her arms over her chest.

"You're not even a little curious what the consequences will be?" I tease. It's nothing compared to what I'm planning in my mind while she considers her words.

"I assume more of the same." She lifts a shoulder, the pretense of boredom shattered by the dilation of her pupils. The silver blue of her eyes makes it so easy for me to see her reaction from where I stand. Poor girl has nowhere to hide.

I slide my hands into my pockets and move to her. She drops her hands to the dresser, gripping the edge. As I inch closer to her, she has to tilt her head back to look up at me.

"You should never assume with me, princess." I grab hold of the belt tied around her waist and untie it. When she moves to block me, I tsk my tongue. "Don't get in my way, princess."

She moves her hands back to the dresser.

"Don't call me that." She grits her teeth.

I finish untying the belt and the robe spreads open.

"No." She tries to twist away from me, but I only have to move forward an inch and I have her trapped.

I pull the robe open more and am surprised to find her nude beneath. A blush creeps up her throat, over her face.

"Do you think you deserve another spanking?" I gently cup her shoulders beneath the satin robe and push it over her arms, until it slides down to the floor. We stand in puddle of lavender satin.

She clenches her eyes shut and turns her face to the side. I bet she didn't think this would be happening when she stepped out of my shower.

"Answer me." I spread my hand over her throat, gently wrapping my fingers around the delicate flesh.

She brings her fiery eyes to mine. The deep blush on her cheeks is a stark contrast to the blue in her eyes. Her breath is shallow beneath my hand. I'm careful not to squeeze, not yet, not until she trusts me not to hurt her.

"Lena," I sigh, brushing the tip of my nose against hers. "Tell me, do you deserve another spanking?"

A muffled sound comes from deep in her chest. Indecision? Should she admit what she wants? Or does she want me to force her?

"I... let me have my privacy, Micah. At least until the wedding." Her whispered plea surprises me but doesn't persuade me.

"That would be lying to you, then." I pull back enough to see her clearly. "I already know, princess. I know about the secret bank account. I know about the secret college classes. I already know."

She swallows beneath my grip. Her breathing picks up; her pulse quickens beneath my fingers.

The color drains from her cheeks, and I let go of her throat.

"Relax." I run the back of my hand down her cheek. She's completely nude, right in front of me, but I have to force myself to ignore it. "Breathe, Lena. I'm not mad. It's not a bad thing what I found. It's not bad." I assure her because I'm certain she's afraid I'm going to ruin all of her secret plans.

"You dug into my personal life?" She raises her chin, closes her eyes, and takes a deep breath. I wait, watching as she works to calm herself, though I'm not sure if she's trying not to panic or trying not to kill me. When her eyes open again, a fire rages in them.

"I'm not a man who goes into situations blind," I explain. "We can talk about why you've kept it all hidden later, but first we should discuss the lies." We will talk about it, but right now, I want her in my bed. I want her spread out and calm. I want to show her things don't have to be harsh between us. We may not have planned our union, but it doesn't have to be a relationship filled with hatred and fear.

"My father would have made me drop the classes if he knew. I only lied because I thought you'd do the same," she tells me. "Can I have my robe back, please?"

Half of my mouth pulls into a grin. "No." I kick the robe away from us, out of reach. "I like you this way, naked and honest."

She presses her lips together.

"Well, since you didn't convince me, and you lied, you'll have to pay the price." I trail my hand down her arm and lace my fingers with hers. "Come." I tug lightly, but she's already in step with me as I bring her to the bed.

"Micah—" It's barely a protest as I gesture to the bed.

"Grab the pillows and make a pile in the middle, then lay over them so your ass is propped up for me," I instruct her as I work the buttons on my shirt open.

"I don't think... this isn't right," she says, but grabs two pillows. "It wasn't really a lie. That book is a book I'm reading."

I laugh. "It was true enough that you escaped a punishment, yes, but you're not getting out of this spanking." I tug my shirt off and toss it onto the chair in the corner. My undershirt lands on top of it. I kick out of my shoes and pull off my socks. She glances at me, standing at the side of the bed in only my black slacks, my hands on my belt.

"You said you weren't going to punish me." Her gaze wanders over my chest, pausing at the scar on my right pec I received the same night I earned the scar on my jaw, before moving across my stomach and then lower still.

"This isn't a punishment, Lena," I say, unbuckling my belt. The jangle of the buckle makes her jump, and I can't help but grin. When I rip it from my pants, the leather zipping across the fabric, her ass clenches. She tucks her bottom lip between her teeth. The signs, so many of them. I wonder if anyone's ever bothered to pick up on them. "You'll see."

"I'm not sure I want to," she mumbles.

I laugh. It's refreshing, a woman who speaks her mind with no ulterior motive. I doubt Lena would know how to manipulate someone even if she wanted to. It's this purity that has me hungering to be inside her, to make her mine.

She dips her chin when I climb onto the bed beside her. Lightly, I stroke her back, petting her from her neck down to the adorable dimples at the base of her spine. Goose pimples pop up in the wake of my touch. I scrape my teeth across my bottom lip, fighting back the urge to lick her, bite her.

The idea isn't to scare her.

Yet.

I lay the length of my belt down her back, leaving the buckle on her ass. With my hand, I rub circles into her ass. There's no marks from her previous spanking. Disappointing, but not surprising. I'd gone easy on her, not knowing how much she could take. But I have a better idea tonight.

With my left hand, I push her head down to the mattress, fisting her hair at the back of her head.

"Micah." The thick comforter muffles her weak protest.

"Shh, just relax," I say to her and lightly spank her ass. She stiffens for a moment, more from surprise I'd guess. When she softens, I give her another playful swat. These don't hurt, but they are preparing her for the ones that will.

"Spread your legs a little for me." I slide my hand between her thighs and pull one leg toward me. Her back arches and her ass raises. Leaning to the side and forward a bit, her pussy is displayed for me. Her lips part with her position. Already she's glistening with her arousal.

I give her another smack to both cheeks, watching as they bounce back into perfect formation. A pink handprint is left behind. That won't do, it needs to be darker.

"You're nicely shaven," I say, then smack her ass again. She groans, but I'm not certain it's embarrassment over my observation or desperation for my touch.

I abandon her ass and slide my hand between her legs, cupping her sex. On instinct, she presses her hips into my touch, seeking out satisfaction. I grin down at the back of her head, where my hand is still holding a fistful of her slick wet hair.

"Not yet," I say more to myself than her, and withdraw my hand. "You're still learning, you'll get your reward later."

She huffs when my hand is gone.

"Reward now, teach later," she taunts me.

I smack her ass hard, leaving a red blotch on her warm skin. She hisses and pulls back from me but I'm not letting her go anywhere.

"I'll decide when you're to be rewarded, princess." I release her hair and drag the belt down the length of her back. Folding it in half, I tuck the buckle in my palm and wrap my left arm around her waist.

"What are you doing?" She tries to get up from the mountain of pillows she's draped over, but I hold her firmly against me.

"Hold still, Lena." I raise the belt and bring it down hard on the upcurve of her ass. She yelps. "One more," I say then give her another lash across her prepared flesh. It's not hurting as much as it would on a cold ass, but I'm being generous tonight.

"Fuck!" She slams her fist into the bed.

"I don't like that language at all." I snap the belt across her ass again and she kicks her foot out. "Should I tie you down?" I'm teasing, but she's not looking at me, so she probably can't tell.

She throws her hands in front of her and fists the comforter. Bringing it up to her face, she shakes her head.

"No?" I snap the leather across her ass again and again. Each time her thighs tense, her ass clenches, and she makes the sweetest mewling sound. Her toes curl in and her legs shift, opening more for me.

I deliver three hard lashes to her ass without any reprieve between them. She cries out when the belt makes contact for the third time and shoves up to her knees. I let go of the belt and grab her shoulders, turning her toward me. Before she can wipe the hair from her face, I grab hold of her face with my hand and cover her mouth with mine.

There's a fire building. A white-hot flame growing larger and brighter with each second of our kiss. She brings up her hands, pressing them to my bare chest, but not shoving me away. She inches closer to me until our bodies are touching, until I can feel the hard peaks of her nipples pressed into me.

I break the kiss, staring down into her eyes; her lips are puffy and well kissed. I want more from her. I want it all.

While keeping our gaze locked, I reach down and shove the pillows toward the head of the bed. Her hands move to my pants, working the button open, pulling down my zipper.

The spanking has her eager for me; her movements are quick, frantic really as she shoves my pants over my hips, taking my boxers with them.

I work my clothes off and let them fall to the floor beside the bed.

"On your back," I order her, my voice raw with my need for her.

She scrambles to the pillows, but she's not fast enough for me. I smack her ass and grab her hips, flipping her to her back in one move. She lands with a soft bounce, a seductive grin tugging on her lips.

Without another direction, she lets her knees fall to the sides, opening for me, welcoming me.

I fist my erection and bring it to her pussy, pushing against her entrance but not entering. Biting the inside of my cheek, I look down at the woman beneath me. Strands of wet hair stick to her cheek, her forehead. Wide eyes stare up at me with a hunger I understand, I feel it too.

"Ask me, Lena. Ask politely." I lean over her body, kissing her chin, her jaw, her ear. "Be sweet about it," I whisper into her ear.

"Micah," she breathes out my name as I push forward into her hot passage enough to feel her pussy clench my cock.

"More. Tell me what you need, princess."

The moniker has her tensing. Every bit of her. I groan as her body grips my cock and I plow straight into her, not stopping until my balls hit her ass and I'm embedded fully inside her.

She sucks in a breath and her nails dig into my shoulders.

I bring my gaze to hers again. "Say it."

For a second I think she's going to argue. She's going to try to prove to me that she will do only what she wants, and she won't give me the submission I want from her.

"Fuck me, Micah." She moves her hands from my shoulders to my face, holding me still as she raises her head from the pillows to get closer to me. "Hard."

I raise an eyebrow.

"Please," she adds.

I grab her wrists and pin them next to her head, holding her to the bed as I pull almost completely free from the hot sheath of her body. In the next instant, I slam into her. She moans, draws her knees up and out.

"Fuck," I groan as her movements tighten her pussy around me. I sink into her again and again, plowing faster and harder, until the sounds of our bodies colliding fills the space between us. She arches her back, grinds her hips up at me to meet each of my thrusts.

"Micah, Micah, Micah," she chants while reaching up to kiss my throat, my shoulder. Her teeth sink into me and it fuels me.

Electric heat trickles down my spine and my balls pull up tight, ready to explode.

Letting go of one wrist, I reach between us until I find the swollen, wet bundle of nerves. The instant my finger brushes against her clit, her eyes snap open.

"You like this? Your little clit played with?" My teasing makes it difficult for me to keep from taking my own release. I circle the nub, around and around, until she's back to crying out my name. Louder and louder she says it.

I flick my fingertip across her clit and plow into her hard enough to shake the bed, and in the next second, she unravels beneath me. She screams my name until the sound fades away.

Her orgasm washes over my cock, hot fluid runs over me, her pussy clenches me. I pump into her again and again and by the third stroke, my own release crashes over me. I still, emptying into her while trying to find air to breathe. My spine tingles; my vision blurs at the edges.

Finally, air fills my lungs. The fog lifts and I can see clearly. Lena lies beneath me, one hand still pinned to the pillow and a satisfied grin spread across her lips. I let her wrist go and blink several times until my thoughts line up in logical order.

My cock slips from her pussy and I move back to my knees. She pulls her knees together, but she can't hide my cum dripping out from her pussy lips. When I drag my gaze back up to her, there's a soft blush on her cheeks.

"Don't go getting shy on me now," I chuckle and climb off the bed.

"I'm not," she says, but contradicts herself by scrambling beneath the covers and pulling them up to her chin. "But can you hand me the robe?"

I pick up the item from the floor and drape it over the chair, out of her reach. "You don't need it."

"I left my nightgown in the dresser." She points to the drawers. "The left side."

"You don't need that either." I grab my boxers from the floor and use them to wipe her juices from my cock. The mental image of making her lick me clean erupts in my mind, and I have to work hard to shove it away.

"Why not?" she asks when I climb into bed beside her.

"No clothes are allowed in my bed, princess." I reach over and flick the light switch on the wall beside the bed, throwing the room into darkness.

She settles under the covers, pulling the pillows close to herself and rolls to her side. With her back to me, I wrap my arm around her middle and drag her across the bed until she's pressed against me. The woman fits me in every way.

She smells of lilacs and coconut. An odd combination, but I inhale it deeply. The soft scents lull me half asleep. It's been a long week, and there's even longer days ahead of us.

"I'm not a princess," she whispers, and I don't think I'm supposed to hear her.

I hug her tightly to me, nudge her shoulder with my chin.

"Maybe you should be."

She stiffens but doesn't respond. I like her this way, soft and pure, and most important—Mine.

CHAPTER 15

ena

It's odd, this sensation of familiarity and calm with Micah sitting across from me at the breakfast table. His housekeeper is here today, and she filled my plate with eggs, bacon, and fresh cut fruit. Everything is delicious, but I didn't have a chance to tell her before she danced out of the kitchen to get to work.

"How often does she come?" I ask him as he sips his coffee. He drinks it black while I shovel another spoonful of sugar and cream into mine.

"Delphia? Three times a week. She'll leave a few prepped meals in the fridge. But I like to cook for myself most of the time." He looks at my plate with a smile. "You have a healthy appetite."

Only a few bites of the strawberries are left. "Are you saying I eat too much?" I try to draw irritation, but the playfulness of his eyes stops me.

"No. It's good." He leans back in his chair. "You slept okay?"

I tense, unsure of what to say about our sleeping arrangement. What happened last night, how easily he turned me into an aroused animal with a few straps of his belt, how can I look at him in the eye this morning?

"Yeah. Good," I say and hide behind my coffee cup, grimacing at the taste. It's still too bitter.

"And you're feeling all right this morning?"

My cheeks heat with his question. He's not even being subtle; the joviality of his voice tells me he finds the entire line of questioning amusing.

"I'm feeling perfectly perfect this morning," I say with a raised chin. I won't let him bait me into an argument. I do feel good this morning. Last night was the best sleep I've gotten in weeks.

"Good to hear," he says with a wink. "About school." He puts his cup down and leans forward. The playfulness is gone and he's back to being all stern and serious.

Of course he's going to demand that I drop it. I'm to be his wife, and the wife of the Bratva doesn't hold a career.

"The next session starts soon, right?"

My gaze flies up to his. There's no dark brooding glare staring back at me, just curiosity.

"Next month, yes." I remain cautious.

"Do you have your classes picked?"

I sink in my chair. If he's giving this to me only to pull it out from me in the next breath, I'm not sure I'll be able to keep myself from shoving my fork into his throat.

"I haven't enrolled yet, no." I hadn't worked out which class to take. If I signed up for more than one, my father might have found out easily.

"Then you can do that this morning. You can do it online, yes?" His eyebrows rise, wrinkling his forehead. His hair is slicked back, and even though he's shaved there's a shadow along his jaw.

I blink away the moment. I can't keep gawking at him; it will only go to his already arrogant head. "Yes. I can do it online."

"Good." He gets up from the table and pulls his jacket from the back of the chair. "Then do it today, sign up for as many as you need." He fixes the collar of his shirt with the jacket on then pulls out his wallet. "Use that." He drops a credit card on the table next to my plate.

I pick up the plastic card. It's a black Amex. No limit. Is he crazy to give this to me?

"You're okay with me going to school? To get a degree?" I run my finger over the edge of the card.

He walks around the table and cups my chin, pulling my attention up to him. "We are different, you and I. We're not like our fathers." He kisses me. Warmth runs from my lips down to my very core. I feel like I'm lifting off the chair and I curl my toes into my shoes to keep from floating away. When he pulls away and I blink my eyes open, he's smiling down at me.

"Also, there's a seamstress coming today with wedding gowns for you to try on and pick. I expect you to find something from what she brings or tell her what you want and she'll have it made."

"By Saturday?" I ask with wide eyes. "That's only three days."

"More than enough time," he says and buttons the jacket of his suit. "Your brother's wife is coming today too."

"What?" I tense beneath his stare. It's overpowering when he directs such fierceness toward me. I'm not sure he means to do it; power just runs through his veins.

I shake my head. "No. I don't want to see her."

He smiles and touches the tip of my nose. "And who asked if you did or didn't?" He grows serious again. "She's your brother's wife. You'll be gracious, and if I find out you weren't, you'll get another taste of my belt that you won't enjoy so much."

"You can't just do that whenever you don't like something. I'm not a little kid."

"I think you'll find that I can do whatever I want, whenever I want with you." He leans over me, caging me with one hand on the back of my chair and the other on the edge of the table. "You have brothers and now you have a sister. Be grateful for them."

A sadness touches his eyes, peeking through the dominant stare he's settled on me. He had a brother, I remember that.

"I don't understand you," I say, searching him for a sign as to who the hell he is exactly. One moment he's nothing more than a powerful man in the Bratva who can and will crush me at his will, and the next he's insisting I continue my education and wants me to build bridges with my family.

"I'm not as complicated as you think." He kisses my forehead. "I have meetings all day. We'll have dinner at the restaurant tonight. Be good to Kasia. Pick a dress and sign up for your classes. If you need to go anywhere, you'll call me first and I'll have someone take you." He pushes away from me, though I can still feel his warmth.

"I don't have your number."

"It's programmed into your phone."

"Along with that tracker?" I ask, giving him a side glance.

"Yes, and the tracker will stay on it."

"You don't need to do that. It's not like I have anywhere I could run if I wanted to run away."

"I'm not worried about you running away." He takes his plate and coffee cup to the sink. "My family has enemies, Lena. As does yours. Snatching the daughter of a high-ranking member of the Staszek family is a good way to hurt your father." The irony of his statement hangs between us. "Kidnapping the fiancée of a high-ranking member of my family is just as lucrative to my enemies. It's for your safety that I know where you are and that one of my men goes with you."

He's right, but I don't concede the point.

"I'd like to get coffee with my friends," I say as his phone dings, taking his attention away from me.

"Let me know when, and Dimitri will be here." He taps away on his phone. "I'll see you at the restaurant eight o'clock."

The seamstress walks through the main hallway of the apartment straight back toward Micah's rooms when she arrives. Her introduction was rushed as she waved the two men pushing the racks of dresses off the elevator.

"Back this way, quickly now," she says and shows them down the hall. Obviously, she's been here before.

Dimitri steps off the elevator right before the doors begin to close on him. He's already frowning. Micah's cousin hasn't been anything but civil with me, but there's a strange sensation that crawls over my skin when he's around. He obviously thinks being my babysitter for the day is beneath him. I would agree with him and send him on his way, but he's one of Micah's men. He'll do what he's told. No matter how unpleasant it probably is.

"Hi. I guess we'll be in the sitting room." I gesture toward the roaming caravan of gowns and turn on my heel to follow.

"Your sister-in-law will be here in a few minutes." Dimitri plops his bulky form into the chair beside the elevator entry. "I'll bring her back when she arrives." He pulls out his phone and begins scrolling through his screen.

Dominik hasn't texted me or called. This visit has been set up through Micah. No matter my age or my station, I'm still the useless girl who has to have everything done for her.

"That would be nice, thank you." I force a pleasant tone, practice for when I have to deal with Kasia. Micah's way of going about gaining my cooperation doesn't frighten me—not after last night. I doubt he could ever make me fear his belt after what he did to me, what I begged for him to do to me. But he did have a solid point. She's my family now, and I should hold on to whatever I can. The Ivanovs can take them away whenever they choose. For now, I'll be grateful for what I have.

When I enter the sitting room, the seamstress—a fifty-something-year-old woman with stick-straight shoulder-length hair—flounces around the room giving her two assistants directions. Put that rack there, move this chaise, bring out the platform. It's a whirlwind of motion, and I stay planted in the doorway and out of the storm.

"Lena?" A gentle hand touches my arm, startling me to her presence.

"Yes." I face her, keeping my hands at my sides. I may have to be civil, but I don't have to hug the woman whose actions have condemned me.

"Hi. I'm Kasia." She fidgets with her purse strap on her shoulder. She's dressed in a long dark brown knit sweater, black leggings, and a pair of black flat boots. Her thick long blonde hair is swept to her right side, wide curls cascade down the sweater. Aside from a light coat of pink lip gloss and mascara that brings out her creamy brown eyes, she's the picture of natural beauty.

No wonder Dominik fell so hard for her.

"Do you have any idea what sort of dress you're looking for?" She moves her gaze to the racks being unpacked to showcase.

My shoulders sag. "I have no idea. Something... plain?" I fold my arms in front of me. "Although I think my father would expect something expensive. Something full of beads and pearls. Maybe some diamonds sewn into the seams."

She looks at me with wide eyes, searching me.

After a long pause, I grin. "What, they haven't filled you in on what a spoiled Polish princess I am?"

Her lips pinch together and her eyes flicker back to the seamstress.

"They haven't said anything like that," Kasia says when the silence stretches between us.

"You don't need to cover for my brother. I know what he thinks of me. I'm impulsive, selfish, and reckless. I don't appreciate everything that they've done for me. I've heard the lectures lots of times growing up."

"Dominik has only said good things about you," she says, but I can hear the edge.

"Dominik has only said that I will do what's right. He's promised you not to worry, that I'll make everything all better because I have no choice." I can't help the bitterness twisting between my words.

"He's said that you've been sheltered, but so was I. Our fathers aren't terribly different when it comes to the values they hold for their daughters. Although I will say your father seems a bit kinder. He does love you, Lena."

The seamstress walks toward us, but I hold up a hand to still her. "Loves me? He's sold me off to the Ivanovs. Is that something a father does to a daughter he loves? I haven't even heard from him since he signed me over to his enemy. I understand you married Dominik because your father was no better in that regard, but you were lucky."

"Lucky how?" She narrows her eyes slightly. Whatever pleasantry we skirted around is gone.

"Dominik is a good man."

"He is, yes. But when I married him, when he came and took me from my home in the middle of the night, I didn't know what sort of man he was. I had no idea what I was getting into. All I was to any of them was a pawn to be moved about. Just like you, and I'm sorry for it." She takes a long breath. "I'm sorry this has happened. I'm sorry it's because of what I did, but I'm not sorry I did it."

I clench my teeth. Dimitri is well within hearing distance, and he'll no doubt report every word back to Micah.

"Those women—" She takes a shaky breath. "The women my father was transporting like cattle were abused. No one should have to go through what those women have gone through. So no. I'm not sorry that I took them from that fate. If I had to do it again, knowing what the consequences would be, I would do the same."

She pulls photographs from her purse and shoves them at me. "Those are the women we rescued that night." She points a finger at them as I take the pile from her. Flipping through them slowly, I see the battered women. Bruises, cuts, old scars litter them beneath the dirt and fear clinging to their faces. My stomach twists, remembering the cries of the women in the stable those few nights I was kept there.

While I was whisked away and given to Micah Ivanov, those women remained. What happened to them after I left? Are they still down there, waiting to be transported, sold into a life of slavery?

I hand the pictures back to her, my throat too full of emotion to speak.

"Micah's father has so many others," I say when I find my voice. I glance down the hall to find Dimitri engrossed with his phone. "You saved them, but there are more."

She puts the photographs back into her purse and folds her arms over her chest. Pain crosses her features.

"I know. It's an argument I have with your brother often. And now they are marrying you into a family that makes their money by selling these women."

"You argue with him? Dominik can't like that." I find a small smile at the image of my brother being argued with by this woman. She's the same size as me, practically a dwarf compared to my brother.

She grins. "He doesn't."

"I don't think Micah wants to keep that part of his father's business," I tell her, keeping my voice low so Dimitri can't hear. I doubt I know anything that he doesn't, but just in case, I don't want to cause a problem between Micah and his father.

"Dominik says the same thing. Micah's taken on a lot of projects outside his family dealings," she says, but a frown still tugs at her lips.

"I was surprised Micah was all right with you coming over today."

Kasia's brows knit together. "It was his idea. He called Dominik this morning."

Micah planned this?

You have brothers and now you have a sister. Be grateful for them.

I'm not sure what to think about this. About him.

"If we are going be done before this afternoon, we should get started." The seamstress claps her hands for our attention.

"Right," I say.

"I know you're angry with me, but I want you to know that you can always call me if you need something. If you want to vent, or cry on a shoulder, or just want someone to throw things with, I'm here." Her words come from a genuine place of kindness, and the last bit of me that was holding on to my anger fades away.

"I don't think I would have done any differently if I was in your shoes." I admit. "I heard the women in that stable, heard them crying, heard their screams when one of the men came for them—" I clear my throat and grab her hands in mine, squeezing. "You did the right thing, Kasia."

She smiles brilliantly, lightening the mood. "It's good to have a sister again."

I squeeze her hands again then turn to the seamstress. "Let's get this over with. What monstrosity do you want me to try on first?"

Kasia laughs, but the seamstress's jaw slacks in shock.

"I'm kidding," I assure her and walk to the first rack. "Do you have something simple? Nothing frilly or goofy. Just something elegant?"

The seamstress grins and throws her hands up in the air with excitement. "I have just the thing!"

CHAPTER 16

$\mathcal{L}$ena

It's eight-thirty by the time Dimitri pulls the SUV up to Micah's restaurant.

"Thanks," I say to Dimitri as I climb out of the car before he can open my door. When I step onto the pavement, he's almost reached me with a dark frown on his face. "Don't worry, if Micah asks, I'll be sure to let him know you opened the doors."

He shakes his head. "You don't do anything you're supposed to do. It's dangerous," he warns me as he pushes my door closed.

"How can it be dangerous when I have Micah and his men protecting me?" I flash him a smile and head into the restaurant.

There's a crowd when I step inside. Business must be good, then. I see a hand burst up over the heads of those standing in front of me, then a woman slightly taller than me gingerly weaves her way through the customers.

"Ms. Staszek, good evening. Right this way, please." She flashes me a bright smile.

I follow her through the crowded entrance and then through the dining room. Laughter mixes with the background sounds of silverware hitting dishes as I'm led around the tables of diners. Warm scents of their meals rise up and my stomach rumbles in reaction.

"Mr. Ivanov is waiting for you in the private room in the back. The chef will bring out your meals directly," the hostess explains as we turn down a corridor. There's a wall of greenery shielding us from the main dining room.

From ahead of us, a door opens and a black-haired woman steps into the corridor, pulling the door closed behind her. She checks her phone, adjusts the strap of her dress, then stalks toward us. When passing, she flashes a grin and a wink. I stop, wanting to take another look. She didn't look familiar, but she seemed to know who I am.

"Mr. Ivanov has been in meetings all afternoon," the hostess says as a way of explaining away the woman maybe.

"He's a very busy man," I mutter and follow her the rest of the way to the same door the mystery woman exited.

"Would you like something to drink? There's a bottle of wine available already in the room, but if you'd like something else, I'll have the bartender bring it over directly."

"No, that's fine. Wine is good," I say.

She nods. "Have a pleasant evening, Ms. Staszek." She leaves me at the door and hurries back down the corridor. Her station's been left empty and from the crowd size, I'd say she's probably going to be met with some angry faces.

When I enter the room, Micah's on the phone pacing the floor. He catches my gaze and stops; his eyes wander down my body then back up. An appreciative smile tugs the corners of his lips.

"Get back to me tonight. I have to go." He clicks off his call before waiting to hear the response from the other end.

I run my hands over my hips. Kasia talked me into wearing this deep purple cocktail dress. The plunging V neckline dips enough that the swell of my breasts invites his stare to linger. The dress hits just above my knee, but the high heels lengthen my legs and give me some height.

Micah drops his phone onto the table on his way to me, his eyes latched onto mine. He prowls the same way I imagine a tiger stalks its dinner. There's a flutter in my stomach at the determination in his eyes, and I want more.

"I'm sorry I'm a little late. Traffic was bad," I say.

He reaches his hand to my chest and picks up the single diamond on my chain. My skin heats where his fingertips touched.

"Dimitri told me." He thumbs the diamond. "Were you a good girl today, Lena?" he asks, dropping my necklace and arching a single eyebrow.

"I ordered a dress if that's what you mean."

"And your classes?" he prompts.

"I registered for three," I answer.

"And your visit with Kasia?" He tilts my head back with his fingers beneath my chin. "You behaved?"

If Dimitri already informed him about the traffic, there's no doubt he's already tattled about my visit with my sister-in-law.

"I did."

The dim lighting in the room casts his face in a shadow, giving him a more dangerous look than normal.

"The hostess said there's a bottle of wine in here?" I say after too many moments tick by and he's still staring down at me ready to take his first bite.

He releases my chin. "There is."

I tear my gaze from him, looking over at the table. The places have already been set on each side of the table that could easily sit eight people. In the center is a tall vase filled with orchids, and two lit candles flank the vase on either side. A bottle of wine sits beside two empty wineglasses next to one place setting. I assume that's where he'll be sitting.

"Were you expecting a romantic dinner?" I ask with a smile when I bring my eyes back to his.

"When I said I wanted this room for us tonight the staff took it upon themselves," he explains. "They did a good job."

"Did you have a good day?" I change the subject. Romance isn't necessary between us, and I won't have him thinking that I'm any more of a princess he already considers me to be.

His eyebrows furrow together. "My day?" he asks as though the question confuses him.

"Yes. Did you have a good day? Your meetings. Work," I repeat. Has no one ever bothered to ask this man about his day?

"It was—productive."

I laugh. "Productive? Is that how you measure your days? If you've moved the needle or not?"

"How else do you suggest I measure it?" He tilts his head, genuinely curious.

I blank for moment. How would a high-ranking member of the Bratva measure his day?

"Did you have to kill anyone today?" I blurt the question.

His eyes go wide, shocked, probably that I had the stupidity to put those words together verbally. Once he recovers from my bluntness, his lips spread wide in a grin that produces a deep crease on the side of his mouth. The scar on his jaw even flickers with his amusement.

"No. No, I didn't," he answers, keeping his smile in place.

"Well, then I'd say you had a good day." I shrug. "As well as everyone else in Chicago."

He laughs; it's a hearty sound, coming from the depth of his chest. Micah grabs my hand and brings it to his mouth where he kisses the inside of my wrist.

"My day was good, then. How was yours?" He leads me to the table, to the chair opposite the wine. I sit down as he holds the chair for me, tucking me in at the table before moving to his seat.

"I've already told you," I remind him. "Can I have a glass?" I point at the wine. He's sitting and not touching it.

He pours a glass for me and pushes it across to me. I have to reach for it but snag it without spilling. When I look back up at him, I catch his eyes fixating on my breasts.

In some ways, boys never stop being boys.

"Thank you." I take a sip of the wine. No matter how many times he's stared me down, every time feels like the first. My nerves might need more than a few sips of the warm red wine.

"You said what you did, you didn't say how it was." He waves his hand in the air and a hidden door behind him opens. Waiters fill the room, bringing us each a plated meal and fresh glasses of water. A basket of warm bread is placed on the table.

The aroma of the plate demands I take in the dish before me.

"Pierogi?" I pick up my fork. They're smaller than I've had before, more round, but they smell similar.

"No. Pelmeni," Micah corrects me. "A meat-filled dumpling."

Heat hits my cheeks at my ignorance. Of course he wouldn't serve a Polish meal at his restaurant.

"Right. It looks delicious," I say, cutting into one of them. My mouth waters.

"So, how did your visit with Kasia go?" He repeats his question.

"It went all right," I answer after I swallow the flavorful bite. "It will be nice to have a sister," I add and take another sip of my wine.

Micah doesn't touch his meal while I devour mine. When I catch him smiling at me, I pause with my fork halfway to my mouth.

"No, no, eat," he says when I start to put my fork down. "I had a late lunch."

I finish the last bite then place my fork over the plate. I could eat three more servings, but I've embarrassed myself enough for one night.

As soon as my fork hits the plate, two waiters rush into the room and clear away our dishes and the untouched basket of bread.

"Dessert?" one of them asks, pausing near Micah.

"Please, no," I say, touching my hand to my stomach.

Micah gives a small shake of his head, and the waiter disappears through the kitchen door. Before the waiter closes the door, he flicks a latch.

"They won't be back until I unlock the door," Micah explains when he catches me staring.

"Everything was delicious," I say as the silence stretches between us. "I can see why you have so many people waiting to get in."

"The reservation bookings are full for the next three months," he tells me.

"Three months? Then what was all that at the front? I thought they were waiting for a table."

"We leave four tables for drop-ins, people wait over two hours to be seated." He grins. "People passing by see the crowd and they are intrigued about the restaurant."

"So, you use customers as bait to drive in more customers." I smile. "That's a good idea."

"It's working well so far."

"And do you think you'll open another restaurant? Out by Dominik there's mostly chain restaurants. Something unique like this could do well."

"I'm hoping to expand, yes." He drums his fingers on the tabletop. "What did you and Kasia talk about this afternoon?"

The question sucks the wind from my lungs. Dimitri wasn't as oblivious to us as I thought. And he's told Micah everything.

"Are you afraid she'll save more women from your father's stable?" The question comes out harsher than I intended, but there's no taking it back.

He narrows his eyes. "I'm afraid of what will happen to my wife if she acts against my father."

"I'm not your wife yet," I remind him.

"You will be in short order, Lena, and I don't want you doing anything against my father. Do you understand?"

"What your family does—" I look away. "It's wrong. Worse than wrong."

His fingers curl into a fist on the tabletop but his expression remains soft. "I will worry about my family business. You will worry about going to school, getting good grades, being my wife, and raising our children."

"Is there a rush for children?" I ask. "Because I can't... I'm not able to become pregnant yet."

"Why is that?"

"I have an implant. It's good for another year."

"You didn't mention it before."

"We haven't had a real conversation about our marriage before," I point out. "We don't even know each other, Micah. Can we not wait for children at least a year?"

He stares at me in silence. His thoughts could be anywhere, but I can't read him. I can't tell what he wants.

"You'll stay away from my father's business dealings? I can't control Kasia, but I will not have you involved." His hand flattens on the table. "I'm asking you to trust me on this, Lena. I know we aren't close yet, but I want your trust. I will handle the stable."

"And you'll give me a year before we try to bring children into this?" It's a horrible deal, and one I'm not entirely sure I can honor. If Kasia has a plan, if she needs help, I'm not sure I'll be able to tell her no. But so far, she has no plans to do anything, so it's a safe deal to strike.

"You'll have a year," he promises me.

"Okay." I nod. "I can do that."

"My father won't hesitate to hurt your family if there's any more meddling. I don't want you caught up in that." Concern underlines his statement, making it easier to concede for the moment.

"Kasia isn't going to do anything, Micah," I reveal. "She only showed me the pictures of the girls she saved that one night. She wanted me to understand why she did what she did."

"And do you?"

I raise my chin. "I do. I would have done the same, I think, in that situation. Those women—" I stop my words before the raw anger returns and I end up fighting with Micah. It's been a good evening. Ruining it now would serve no purpose.

Micah's chair moves smoothly across the floor as he rises. Walking toward me, he pins me in place with another hungry stare. When he reaches me, his fingertips run along my jaw, capturing several strands of my hair that he tucks behind my ear.

"You're much stronger than I anticipated." His admission surprises me. "More willful but not in the brat sort of way I expected." He gently picks up my hand and helps me up from my seat, pulling me close into his chest.

"You did call me a brat at first," I remind him.

He laughs. "I thought for sure you were a spoiled brat. But I was only going off rumors; now I have the real thing in my hands I can see that's not the case." He trails one finger along my jaw, then down to my shoulder.

"Because I speak my mind, that's why people think I'm a brat. They think I should be quiet and follow orders like a good little girl." I enclose his finger in my hand and bring it to my mouth. "But that's not me." I wrap my lips around the tip of his finger and gently suck.

His jaw tightens and a low rumble crawls up from his chest. I don't bother hiding my victorious grin as I pull his finger out of my mouth, dragging it across my lips.

"You shouldn't tease me, Lena." He rips his finger from my grip and snatches my wrist, yanking me into his chest.

I tilt my head back as far as I can to look up at him. "Who said I'm teasing?"

His chest vibrates with an animalistic growl. "Go to the door and lock it so we won't be disturbed by anyone accidentally walking in here," he directs me, spinning me away from him. The waitstaff can't come in through the kitchen, but someone could come in from the hallway.

"Lock it?" I wrinkle my forehead.

He smacks my ass. "That's what I said."

Maybe I've bit off more than I can chew with my teasing, but the heat spreading across my body is too inviting to ignore. I make my way to the door, making sure to keep my steps slow and graceful.

"Stay there," he says after I've flicked the lock on the handle. I cross my arms over my chest and stick out a hip.

Micah pulls a chair from the table and flips it around so he's facing me. He makes a show of pulling off his jacket and draping it over the back of the chair. Easily, he unbuttons his sleeves and rolls them up to his elbows.

My ass twitches in remembrance of the last time he prepared himself like this.

"You said yourself I was good today," I say, cringing inwardly at my own voice. I shouldn't be so willing to let him punish me at his will, but if he were to crook his finger at me now and tell me to lie over his lap, I would.

He finishes with his sleeves and scoots his ass up on the seat, hooking his thumbs into his belt.

"You were a good girl, and now I want to see if you're going to make good on your tease, or not." He eyes the floor before my feet. "Get on your hands and knees, Lena, and crawl to me. Show me that you can be my obedient good girl. Not for anyone else, but for me."

My cheeks erupt in flames at the suggestion, but it takes only a moment's hesitation before I'm doing exactly as he's instructed. I pull up the hem of my dress to keep it from getting in the way as I sink down to the floor. I inhale a slow breath, then raise my chin until my gaze locks on his.

One hand forward, then my knee, then my hand again, I crawl inch by inch toward this man who looks ready to devour me if I get too close. I can't deny how wet I am by the time I arrive at his leather loafers. His legs are spread, and he looks down through them at me.

I inch closer, between his thighs, toward the part of him I want now. His hands still cover his belt.

"Open your mouth, Lena. Show me you're ready for me, ready to suck my cock."

His words are crude and crass, and exactly what makes my body respond. I lean back onto my heels and open my mouth for him.

"Good girl," he smiles, and there's that crease again. It gives him a playful charm, but I won't misunderstand it as weakness. This man can take whatever he wants; I don't forget that.

He works his belt open quickly, pulling his zipper down and opening his pants in front of me. He shoves his pants and boxers down, letting them fall to his ankles. I maneuver to fit between his knees and not kneel on his discarded slacks.

With a fist around his cock, he reaches the other hand out to my head, touching me lightly. I don't need any more hints; I lean forward and wrap my lips around his thick head. I smile as the hiss of his pleasure hits my ears.

"Hands behind your back, princess," he says, and for the first time it comes out as an endearment instead of an insult. I fold my hands together behind my back and bob down on his cock. He's long and thick; he fills my mouth and hits the back of my throat before I've reached the base of his cock.

"Swallow," he says, pushing my head further down until I choke. "No." His gentle touch turns into a firm fist in my hair as he holds me down on his cock. "Swallow and take me, Lena. All the way."

Tears prick my eyes as I swallow him down, breathing through my nose, and desperately struggle not to gag on him. Inch by inch, I get more of him down my throat. As I swallow again, the coarse curls at the base of his cock tickle my nose.

"*Blyad*," he groans. *Fuck*. I don't know many words in his language, but that one I'm familiar with. "So good, baby." He lets me up but only for one deep breath before he pushes me back on his cock.

"Again, princess. Swallow me whole." He shoves harder, faster this time and I have to quickly work to accommodate his size in my throat. Once he hits the back of my throat, he drops his grip from my hair.

I bob down on his cock again, licking the underside of his dick as I make my way down, and sucking hard as I withdraw. His hands move to the side of my face.

"Hold still," he orders, his voice raw. I stop moving, but it's only a moment before he's thrusting upward at me. Fucking my throat from beneath me. I swallow as best I can, open for him as tears roll down my cheeks.

I grip tighter on my wrist behind me to keep from reaching forward.

Harder and faster he thrusts, and I steel myself for his impending orgasm. For the hot ropes of his cum that will spray my mouth, down my throat.

But it's not to be.

He yanks from my mouth, pushing me gently back as he sucks in deep breaths. He curses again in Russian, but I don't know these words. Glancing up at his expression, I can see he's frustrated. I run my tongue over my lips, gathering the strings of saliva that have escaped.

"Come here, princess." He reaches down and helps me to my feet. With my hands still behind me and still wearing my heels, I need his assistance, so I don't fall on my face—or his.

His large, warm hands glide up my legs, beneath my dress until he reaches my panties. Hooking his thumbs into the elastic band, he drags them back down, letting them fall to my feet.

"Step out," he says, watching me obey him. I think it makes his cock even harder.

Once my panties have been properly discarded, he pushes my dress up over my hips, exposing me completely to his view. I close my eyes and turn away. Last night was somewhat easier because his gaze didn't linger.

"How wet are you?" he asks, looking up at me, his finger poised to slip between the folds of my pussy. My clit pulses at the thought of his touch.

"Very," I say, running my tongue over my now dry lips.

He brings his knees together and fists his cock again. It glistens with my saliva still.

"Ride me, princess. Keep your hands where they are," he orders when I start to move them.

My shoulders burn, but I'm not ready to chance disobeying him, so I keep them where they are. I step forward, straddling his lap, lining his cock up with my aching pussy.

"Down." He grips my hip and guides me down onto his cock. I stretch around his head, and I pause for a moment. He feels bigger this way. "Down," he says again, moving his hand from my hip to smack my ass.

"It's hard like this," I say, but he shows no mercy.

"Then let me help." Once the tip of his cock is inside me, he grabs my hips with both hands and yanks me down onto his lap. Instantly I'm full of his dick, and I groan, the sound clawing its way out of my throat.

"There." He's breathing harder. At least I'm not the only one affected.

I glance at the door where the waiters came through earlier. "The staff."

"They know better than to come in if the doors are locked," he assures me and lifts my hips, showing me what he wants. And the moment he slams me down back on his lap and my clit brushes the rough curls at the base of his cock, I don't need his help anymore.

"*Blyad*, yes. Just like that, princess." He throws his head back as I ride him, moving faster up and down on his cock. My thighs tremble, my belly tightens, and my cunt constricts around him.

I'm so close to the edge, I forget about my hands and throw them forward, grabbing onto his shoulders as I ride him like the beautiful specimen he is. But he won't have it. He grips my wrists and pries them behind me. Lifting from the chair, he matches my movements and he's fucking me just as hard as I'm fucking him.

Everything inside of me shakes. My heart is in my throat pounding.

"Lena." He leans forward and bites my throat. The sharp prick shoots electric jolts straight to my core and I'm flying so close to the sun, I'm going to burn up.

"Micah! Micah!" I cry out his name, chasing after what he will give me, what I want him to give me.

But he's not done with me.

As I ride him, he slips his hands down my ass, spreading my cheeks far apart. I freeze.

"Have you ever been fucked here?" He taps a fingertip to my asshole.

I blink, sure I heard him wrong.

"Have you ever been fucked in the ass, Lena?" he asks again, the playful smile dangling from his lips.

"N-no, Micah." I dig my nails into my wrist. His mind works for a long beat. With another thrust upward, he grins wide. Before I can catch up to his movements, his finger pushes through my tight muscle and he's in my ass.

I tense, but he's not letting me have a moment to process. As it is, the burn, the stretch adds to the white-hot fire burning in my stomach. Each stroke as he fucks my ass with his finger drives me closer and closer to the flames that will consume me.

"On our wedding night," he announces, thrusting up at me. "I'll take your last bit of virginity. I'm going to fuck your ass, Lena." He shoves his finger further into my ass, filling me, as he makes his declaration. "You'll be truly mine then."

I grind my hips against him, chasing after the impending explosion.

"Say it," he orders me.

"I'll be yours. Truly yours." My thighs burn but I ride him harder, faster. It's so close. "Please," I beg.

He bites my neck again and curls his finger inside my ass. A spark flickers, another and another until my entire body shakes with my release.

"Micah, Micah, Micah!" Each time I say his name a new wave of ecstasy washes over me. Every nerve ending in my body splits into two, sending shockwaves of pleasure through my body, sending my mind into a tailspin.

Slowly, the pleasure fades into a warm hum, and my vision focuses on Micah. He's grinning—proud of himself I'm sure.

He bucks up at me, slipping his finger from my ass to grab my hips. Holding me in place, he thrusts into me over and over again, and I take each pump of his cock with a new arousal beginning to flicker to life. Over and over again he fucks me until his own release sweeps him away.

With a grunt, he falls forward, his head tucks into the crook of my neck. His cock twitches inside me as streams of his hot cum spray into me.

Slowly, I let my arms come forward and wrap them around him. His warm breath rushes over my shoulder as the grip of his release lessens.

He pulls back from me, looking up at me as though he's unsure how we got there. It only lasts a moment before he sits back in the chair and cups my face.

"Such a good girl," he says and brings me to him for a kiss. Less possessive than before but filled with just as much passion. My lips tingle from his touch when he releases me.

"Can you hand me a napkin," I say after another moment passes in silence.

He throws me another devilish smile. "No. Put your panties back on. My cum can soak your panties, your dress, and your thighs for the rest of the night."

"Rest of the night?"

His grin widens, showing off his perfectly white teeth. "I'm suddenly very hungry. I think I'll have dinner now while you sit in your chair."

Before I can argue, he leans to the side and swipes my panties from the floor. They dangle on a single finger between us.

"Micah, they'll know," I say as I take them.

He nods. "Yeah, probably. I don't give a fuck." He sweeps my hair behind my ear again.

I pinch my lips together. "You're impossible."

He laughs. "So are you. We'll make a good pair, yet."

I can't help but feel a balloon of hope begin to fill in my chest. Maybe Kasia was right. Maybe this isn't the worst thing that could happen to me.

Maybe everything will be all right.

CHAPTER 17

M icah

It's five o'clock when we arrive at my father's estate for the celebration dinner. The house is already buzzing with guests when I escort my fiancée inside. At seeing the amount of people milling about in the living room, she steps closer to me and slips her hand into mine.

I give her a squeeze. She has nothing to fear here, but it's understandable she'd be nervous. None of her family or friends are here; my father forbade it. Another way he aims to make Lena uncomfortable, and hopes somehow this will hurt her family.

Roman's old-fashioned ways of doing things don't work the way they used to. Joseph Staszek wants peace; he just wants to do business without worry of constant retaliation. But Roman doesn't think this way. My father is myopic. It will have to be addressed soon.

"Who are all these people?" Lena asks as I lead her down the hall to the winding staircase that will take us up to our rooms.

I glance around at the faces. The sneers I see on some of their faces when they notice Lena send an angry shiver through me. She is to be my wife, and if anyone does anything to hurt her, they will have to deal with me.

"Some family, friends, my father's associates." I step up onto the stairs and tug her along. "Let's get you upstairs and away from them all until we're needed."

She follows me, but glances back down the stairs. "Aren't we needed now?"

"Dinner won't be for another hour or two. You can change and get ready up in our rooms."

Once we step onto the landing, she tugs me to a stop. "I'm already dressed." She looks down at the dark brown dress she's wearing. Her hair is plaited into a thick braid then wound around into a heavy bun at the nape of her neck, showing off her delicate ears. I wouldn't mind skipping the entire show to have a few minutes to nibble on them.

"You picked out two dresses with the seamstress."

"Yes, but I thought the other was for the reception tomorrow night," she explains with a frown. It dawns on me that she has had no involvement in this wedding planning at all. While some women deal with every minute detail of their wedding, Lena has been denied every step.

I bring her to the rooms we'll be using while staying with my father. One night. It's all I'll put up with. After the wedding, I'm taking my wife home.

Once we're inside the seating area of our suite, I lock the door.

"There won't be a reception," I inform her. "Just a small luncheon."

She pushes a half smile onto her lips. "I suppose taking a Polish girl for your wife isn't much to celebrate." The statement lacks sincerity.

"Don't go getting soft on me, princess." I squeeze her hand then let go, showing her the rest of the suite. "There's a bedroom through that door." I point to the right of the sitting room. "Our bedroom is through that door." I spin on my heel and point to the room on the left. "Each bedroom has an attached bathroom. The seamstress will be here in the morning to help you dress."

"I can dress myself," she says softly.

I grin. "I'm sure the dress needs a few pairs of hands for hooks and zippers. Let her help."

"Kasia will be here too."

My eyebrows rise. "Good. That will be good." She needs someone on her side tomorrow. Plus, it will keep Kasia away from my father. He doesn't need another reason to make a scene tomorrow, and it will be difficult day for Lena—I won't add to it by letting my father loose on her family.

"The dress for tonight is in the bedroom." I open the double doors and gesture for her to follow me.

"Your father has a beautiful home," she says as she steps into the bedroom. She wanders to the dresser where family photos are lined up.

"That's Igor." I step behind her and point to the photo she's holding. "My older brother."

"He's handsome." She puts the photo down. "Imagine, if he were still here, I'd be marrying him instead?" she teases with a little laugh, but quickly covers it with her hand. "I'm sorry, that was insensitive. I didn't mean to be rude."

I grab her wrist and spin her around to face me. With my fingertips I brush away little stray hairs from her cheeks and kiss her forehead.

"You weren't rude," I assure her. "And if Igor was still here, you probably wouldn't be here at all. He would have protected that shipment. He would have been more involved in that business and my father wouldn't have even tried to work with the Polish."

She tilts her head to the side. "You think it's a bad thing that you've distanced yourself from that part of your father's world?"

I glance back at the photograph. "Igor was a strong leader. He was raised to be my father's heir while I was raised to have a mind for business."

With a featherlike touch, she brushes her fingers across my jaw. "You're a good man, Micah." She pinches my chin in the same manner I've done with her dozens of times, and I give her the moment. "As good as a man can be in the world we live in. Did Igor agree with your father about—the girls?"

I gently tug her hand away from my chin. "He was not as passionate about it as my father." It's all I'll tell her. Niko has given me hints into my brother's thoughts that make me believe he might have been more against my father's plans than I could have imagined.

"You'll do what's best for your family. And you can do it without the stable." She says the word as though it burns like acid on her tongue.

I grab her by the back of her neck and drag her to me. She flattens her hands against my chest, stabilizing her stance, tilting her face up toward me. She knows what I want, and she wants it, too.

Moving up on her toes, she brushes her lips across mine. When she lowers herself, she's smiling up at me, proud of herself I'm sure for being so bold. It's that action that triggers the most animalistic growl from my chest.

Her smile broadens and I kiss those full lips of hers, tasting the berry flavor of her lip gloss. She wraps her arms around my waist, holding me as I deepen the kiss. Leaning into me, she opens to me, trusting me. It's a drug, her trust. I began this whole thing with her as an order from my father. A job to humiliate our enemy, but here I am kissing her and not wanting to stop. I hold her against me, wanting to protect her and shield her from anyone who might do her harm.

I break the kiss, pressing my forehead to hers and gently rubbing my nose against hers. Our quickened breath mingles between us, as we stand in silence. I can't put words to the emotion building inside of me. I only know that I want more of it and would kill to keep it.

"I have to meet with my father before dinner," I say, reluctantly pulling away from her.

She brushes her hand across her cheek and raises her chin. "I guess I'm supposed to stay here until I'm called?"

"Would you stay if I told you to?" I ask playfully.

She lifts a single shoulder. "I'm not sure, really. It is a big estate, and I could probably wander a bit before someone stopped me."

My father's men would stop her the second she stepped off the stairs, but I don't want to tempt her to test it.

"Then be good for me. Not because I'm ordering you to stay here, but because it will please me if you obey me in this." If my men heard me be so gentle in my approach, they'd probably demand my balls on a platter.

But Lena isn't one of my soldiers. She's to be my wife. I will always expect obedience, but she's not someone to be crushed. She's not my enemy.

Contrary to what Roman thinks.

She hooks her hand into my pants, tugging on the buckle of my belt. "And what prize do I get for being a good girl for you?"

"Careful with your teasing," I warn her with a smile, dragging her hand down to my erection.

Her bottom lip is trapped between her teeth.

"Be a good girl and I'll make you feel good. Be naughty and you won't be sitting at the luncheon tomorrow."

"Or you could make me feel good now—incentive to be good later." She reaches up and kisses my cheek.

I force myself to step back and pull away from the very temptation I can't deny.

There isn't much time before dinner, and I need to talk with Niko before I talk with my father. "Incentive is the reward, princess."

She sighs. "Fine. What time do I need to be downstairs?"

"I'll come get you so we can walk down together." There will be less intimidation with me at her side.

"Okay then." She saunters away and plops down on the bed. "I'll just sit here until you come fetch me."

Her exaggerated sigh makes me grin. She may look playful and sweet now, but I have no doubt if pricked, this woman could pull the heads off her enemies.

"You do that, princess." I adjust my cock. Good or bad, I'm fucking her once we're alone tonight. Her behavior will only determine how much she enjoys it.

I move toward the double doors. "Be good, Lena. I'm serious. Control your temper and your mouth tonight. No matter what my father does or says, or anyone else, don't let them climb under your skin."

She screws up her lips to the side and shrugs.

It's the best I'm going to get without provoking her and time is not on my side.

I shake my head and shut the doors behind me.

If only I could keep her locked in there all night. It's really the only surefire way to be certain she doesn't cause trouble.

Keeping her chained down would be a good option, too. I force myself to stop imagining her body laid out for me with arms and legs tied to the posts of the bed.

The more I think about sinking my cock into her, the more fevered my prayer that she behaves tonight.

"You're sure?" I rub my temples. A heavy throb has taken root ever since Niko started talking. As soon as I'd stepped off the stairs, he'd grabbed me for a private conversation.

"I wouldn't be coming to you with this if I wasn't positive." He wipes his hand across his mouth.

"And you've found her?"

"Micah. Niko. Here you are." My father bursts into the library where we've hidden away to have a private conversation. "We have guests. You should be talking with them, mingling." He closes the door, keeping his back to it and blocking our exit.

"Niko was just giving me some information I asked him for. We were just about to go out." I move from my position near the writing desk, but my father's eyes narrow on me.

"What information?"

"Restaurant related." I wave my hand to clear the suspicion from the room. I've never lied to my father before, not even as a child was I so brave. But until Niko and I can finish this conversation, I'm not bringing my father into it.

He flicks his gaze to Niko, who nods in agreement with me, before finally relaxing his stance.

"You can deal with the restaurant later. Right now, I want a quick word with you before we go out."

"I'll see you at dinner," Niko says as he heads to the door, but Roman stops him.

"Go fetch the Polish girl. Bring her to the dining room; I have the guests being seated now. I want her brought in once they are all comfortable."

KEPT BY HIM

"I'll escort her to dinner," I interject, but my father shakes his head.

"No. Niko will bring her down in fifteen minutes. You will already be in your seat."

"What are you planning?" I ask him.

"Go, Niko." My father waves him away and opens the door for him.

"What's going on?" I ask as soon as the door shuts.

"I have the same question for you." His eyes narrow again, giving him a wary appearance. The longer I look at him, the more aged he seems. Deep wrinkles line his cheeks; his hair is lighter, thinner. Heavy bags rest under his eyes.

"What do you mean?"

"I told you I what I wanted for that Staszek girl. I want her father and her brothers to reek of humiliation when they come tomorrow. Instead, you have her signing up for college? She's going out for coffee with friends? She's living a charmed life with you down there in the city."

"You're having me watched?" Anger burns my chest. Which of my men have been tasked with babysitting me?

"You will do what I ask, Micah. You will make them pay for what they've done." Spittle collects at the corners of his mouth and as he talks it falls.

"She's to be my wife. Her humiliation is mine as well," I point out. "You would have me make her sit in the house all day staring at the walls? For what purpose?"

"Because it's what she deserves!" he yells.

I take a moment to breathe. Lena deserves many things from this life, but retribution for the acts of others is not one of them.

"She's done nothing to you or to me. She's taken this entire situation with more grace than I could have hoped."

"She ran away from you the first night. Is that what you call grace?"

"Lena went to a club."

"She went to her brothers' club! Jakub Staszek is trouble. You need to keep her away from him."

I can't keep up with his orders or his reasoning.

"Niko will have Lena down here any minute. If you want me positioned at the table when he does, we should get in the dining room with the rest of the guests."

"You will not undermine me tonight, Micah." He points a finger at me. His cheeks are blotched with red, and his lips have curled into a pale thin line.

"It's a celebration dinner," I say. "Lena will behave herself and we'll get through this. Tomorrow I'll marry her. The Staszek mess will be done with."

He drops his hand and huffs. "And when she gives birth to your heir and they have to watch him brought up in our family, with our name, our blood in his veins, they'll be sick to their stomachs watching from the outside."

I pause in my step. "What does that mean?"

"After tomorrow, she won't be seeing her family again. She will be an Ivanov, no longer one of them." He yanks the door open and walks out before the words sink in, but once they do my hands close into tight fists.

"What is your obsession with the Staszek family? We've held a peace with them for years. They fucked up our shipment, I get that, and they've more than paid for it. Why are you so hell bent on ruining them this way? Do you want to provoke an all-out war with the Polish? Joseph Staszek is a small part of a much bigger problem we would have."

"Igor would understand." The exasperation in his voice grates against my already on edge nerves.

"Would he?" I challenge.

He puffs out his chest, seeking dominance between us. He holds the power, I won't challenge that, but I won't cower in the shadow of the dead anymore.

"Maybe you should explain it to me then, since I'm here and he isn't."

In three steps he's in my face. "Your brother built me an empire. The Staszek family is getting in the way of it. If you can't see that, if you can't see our enemies then maybe we have a problem."

"And Lena is our enemy too?"

"Once she's firmly put in her place, she'll earn her place in our family. I expect you to keep her on a much tighter leash than you have so far, Micah." He tugs on the lapel of my jacket. "Don't disappoint me, son." A dark warning hangs off his words.

"Did Igor ever disappoint you?" I can't recall a minute of my life that Igor didn't put the sun in the sky for my father.

"Your brother was a good man. He would have put his family above everything." He backs off a step and adjusts the cuffs of his shirt. "Now. Let's get back to our guests."

Hopefully, Lena will be better at hiding her emotions tonight than my father.

CHAPTER 18

ena

Niko looks over his shoulder for the second time as we descend the staircase. I throw on a smile for his benefit, but truth be told my stomach is shaking so hard I might not be able to get anything into it. At least I'll have Micah beside me. I can get through this with him at my side.

"Everyone's already seated," Niko tells me as we arrive at the dining room doors. Sounds of soft laughter and conversation are muffled behind the door. "Are you ready?"

The way he asks gives me pause. It's just a dinner, but something in his tone makes it sound like I'm about to be strung up.

I run my hands down my stomach and hips; the beading of the dress is coarse against my palms. The dressmaker took the waist in just enough to let me breathe comfortably, but still, I can already feel my breath catching. Niko staring at me with such concern isn't helping.

"I'm fine, Niko. Let's go before Mr. Ivanov gets angry." I wave a hand at the door where he's already turning the knob.

He gives me a supportive smile and slides the doors open, revealing a full dining room. He was right, everyone is already in their seats on either side of the long banquet table. Roman Ivanov sits at the head with Micah beside him. The conversation comes to an abrupt stop as soon as I step foot into the room.

Roman keeps his expression bland, but it's still enough to send a chill through me. I take a slow breath, calming myself. As soon as I get to my seat, I can hide beside Micah.

I take a step in the direction of Micah's side of the table, but Niko gently grabs my elbow.

"This way, Lena," he says quietly.

My heart jumps into a rapid race, but I force myself to move with Niko. He takes me around the table, and I do my best to give a smile to everyone staring at me. No one speaks to me, and not a single person smiles in return.

I search the table again for Micah, hoping to find encouragement in his eyes. But my gaze lands on a woman.

The same woman from the restaurant a few nights ago. My heart dives to my stomach. She's seated beside Micah and she's smiling brilliantly at me.

When my gaze drags to Micah, he has a stern set to his jaw.

"Here you are." Niko pulls out the chair for me. I'm seated across from the mystery woman, but thankfully not beside Roman. Niko takes that seat. It's a small comfort, minuscule really considering her hand inches closer to Micah's on the table. Subtlety doesn't appear to be her strength.

"Well. Now that we're all here." Roman nods at the servers waiting in the corners of the room. He hasn't introduced me, and there will certainly be no congratulatory speech on our behalf.

The room fills with conversation once again as the servers begin to bring out the first course. Red borscht. A soup that normally would make my mouth water, but tonight my stomach is too twisted to be accommodating for anything.

"Micah, it's your favorite," the woman says with a singsong voice as she lays her hand on his forearm. "Do you remember the batch I made for us in New York?" She laughs. Her hand wraps around him, squeezing. "It was a disaster."

Micah gives her a warm smile, then turns to his soup. I stare at him. He hasn't even acknowledged my presence. No one, other than Niko, has. My chest cramps watching her lean into Micah, saying something softly and laughing again.

Micah tips his gaze up to me, and I'm frozen as he says something back to her.

"Your soup." A server places a bowl in front of me. My hands stay cemented in my lap. If he's trying to make me jealous it won't work. He can laugh and flirt with whoever he wants to.

"It's made with beets." Niko leans over to me.

I break my stare with Micah. "What?"

He points at the borscht. "The soup. It's made with beets," he says again.

I blink several times. "I know what it is. We have a similar dish." As I turn back to my bowl, I catch Roman glaring at me. It's as though my sheer presence at his table has angered him.

Maybe I should tell him I don't want to be here anymore than he wants me, but something tells me Micah would take exception to that. Though the idea does make me smile as I pick up my spoon.

"Oh, we're ignoring poor Lena," the woman beside Micah says with such a force of fake sympathy I want to pick up the butter knife and shove it in her throat.

I smile instead, putting my spoon back down.

"I'm Katina." Her ruby red lips pull into a bright smile, showing off her perfectly white teeth and a small dimple in her right cheek. Two thick black curls frame her porcelain face. The woman is a picture of perfection. I'm no wallflower myself. I'm not threatened by the beauty of another woman, but the way she leans closer to Micah has my nerves on edge.

Is there something going on with them? They are being so open, so blatant in front of everyone at the table. Sets of eyes wander toward us.

This is meant to be a humiliation. Roman Ivanov wants me to melt into a puddle of embarrassment. Is this the reality of my future with Micah—to sit and watch as he's openly intimate with other women? I'll be forced to be humiliated at every event, every dinner. People will laugh at how foolish I am.

"Nice to meet you," I say when I finally find my voice. "That's a very unique necklace. Very pretty."

She picks up the charm hanging around her neck, dipping almost entirely into her heavy cleavage. Two golden hearts overlap each other and in the center is a setting of diamonds and emerald flecks.

"Thank you, it's one of my favorite pieces." She reaches over and squeezes Micah's hand. "Micah gave it to me for Christmas one year. He had it specially made."

The air whooshes out of my lungs as my heart squeezes. When I drag my gaze to Micah for confirmation, a stormy glare looks back at me.

"For a long time, it was almost certain Katina would marry Micah." Roman says, drawing my attention to him. Others at the table have quietly gone back to pretending not to witness this mess.

"That was a long time ago," Micah says, averting his gaze momentarily to his father. The tension clings to his jawline.

"Not so long." Roman waves a hand. "But," he narrows his eyes on me, "things change."

"Yes, they do," Katina sighs sadly.

"Well, I hope it's not me getting in your way." I force myself to keep my stare on Micah, whose eyebrows shoot up when he turns his attention back on me. "By all means, if you'd like to have him back, I'm sure he and his father can arrange for that. They're very good at arranging the future for women. Deciding who they should be given to."

Niko groans beside me. The man to my left—who no one felt necessary to introduce—gasps. Other guests still their tongues. Silverware stops clinking against their bowls.

"Lena." My name is filled with warning as Micah shoots it across the table at me.

"Truly, Micah." I place my spoon onto the table and tuck my napkin beside my bowl. "I don't want to stand in your way. Of course, I'm sure her father might want to discuss this. Make a good bargain. I doubt he'll sell for a high price given the situation, but I'll leave that up to your family."

"Enough!" Roman's fist pounds into the table, making his soup bowl dance. Droplets of the deep red broth sink into the white linen tablecloth.

Katrina's hot glare settles on me. "How dare you speak so disrespectfully," she says.

"I speak only the truth." My chest is heavy, air gets harder and harder to grab, but I'm not going to let them see my distress. "If it is upsetting, maybe you should discuss the matter with them." I point to Roman and Micah.

"Lena." Again, there's a warning, heavy and unrelenting. "Watch your words."

"I am." I force a grin and curl my toes into my shoes enough to distract my nerves from showing in my voice. "I've been watching how much she clearly wants you and now I'm giving her what she wants. What you obviously want, and what will make your father happy."

"Niko," Roman snaps. "Take Lena to her room. My son will be up to deal with her shortly."

"No." Micah tosses his napkin onto the table and moves to his feet. Katina shifts away from him as he stands. "I'll take her."

I stare at him, frozen in my chair. I've played all my cards. Provoked the beast in him. His lips are pressed thin, his jaw tight as a violin string.

No sense in letting up now.

I push away from the table and sigh heavily.

"You'll have to excuse me; Micah needs a word in private," I say to the table. "I'm sure you'll all enjoy your meal, and I look forward to having you at the ceremony tomorrow." I clasp my hands in front of me as Micah moves around the table. The lion stalking the wounded prey. "That is if Mr. Ivanov isn't able to come to a better offer from Katina's father."

"Lena, stop it." Micah's hand wraps tightly around my forearm and he pulls me away from my seat.

"I do hope you all have a wonderful evening." I wiggle my fingers at them as Micah marches me from the room.

My last sight is Katina's wide-eyed stare on me as I leave. If I'm not imagining things, there's a hint of admiration in her dark brown eyes.

As soon as we're outside the dining room and the doors are closed, Micah pulls me close to him.

"What were you thinking?" he seethes.

I yank on my arm, but his grip only tightens. "Let me go. I'll go upstairs and you can go back to your girlfriend."

He spins me to face him just at the bottom of the staircase. "You've embarrassed my father in front of his men, our family. You're lucky Katina's family isn't here, they would demand retribution for your words."

I stare at him, trying to find an ounce of the man I'd spoken with before he went to his meeting with his father. All I see now are dark, angry eyes.

"No need for retribution." I jerk on my arm again and get free. "You can marry Katina tomorrow and then all will be well."

Without waiting for another word from him, I pick up the hem of my dress and hurry up the stairs. I hear him rushing behind me, but it doesn't stop me. I need to get away from him. To be alone and process my own stupidity.

Of course they will expect some sort of retribution. I challenged and insulted them.

I shove through the main door to our suite and try to run to the bedroom to the right, but Micah's too fast. His arm wraps around my waist, lifting me from the floor. No amount of kicking gets me free. He merely carries me to the door and locks it before bringing me to his bedroom.

"Micah, just leave me." I shove at his arm, but he won't budge.

"I told you, Lena. I told you to behave yourself. I warned you not to let them get to you." He brings me to the bed and dumps me onto the plush mattress. When I look up again, he's standing at the edge, his hands fisted on his hips.

"I won't allow you to humiliate me. I will not stand by watching you have a mistress right in front of my face." I kick out at him, my heel hits his thigh, but he still doesn't budge.

"You're jealous?" He reaches down and grabs hold of my foot, peeling off my heel and dropping it to the floor. Then he grabs my second foot and does the same.

"You can do whatever you want, but I won't let you try to humiliate me. I won't do it."

He runs his tongue along his teeth beneath his lip as he glares silently down at me. After a long pause, he grabs the lapels of his jacket and jerks it off his shoulders.

"Come here." He crooks his finger at me. There might as well be a neon sign over his head blinking *danger*.

"Your father expects you back downstairs," I remind him.

"He expects me to deal with my rude fiancée. And if I go down there right now, they will all know that I didn't deal with your behavior, which will only insult them more."

"Oh." I maneuver myself to the other edge of the bed and get back to my feet, placing the California King between us. "So you don't want to go down there looking less of a man because you didn't make me regret my words?"

His eyes narrow and his bottom lip half-slips between his teeth. I think he's trying to control his temper, but I'm not helping.

"I don't care what they think, but I do care what you think. And right now, you have two very wrong ideas. One, you've gotten it in your head that I'm going to be unfaithful and will wave a woman in your face. You can't be more wrong."

"I suppose Katina is just a friend then? Not your long lost fiancée?"

"Katina was invited by my father."

"She was at your restaurant the other night," I point out.

He nods. "She was. Her cousin works for my father, he brought her to the restaurant for dinner. She came to say hello. After that I sent her away. I hadn't seen her in two years, Lena."

The tension in my chest eases a bit. "Two years?"

"Yes. My father had her come tonight as a way to piss you off, to try and humiliate you—yes, I know what he was trying to do. And I told you not to fall for anything that happened. I warned you to keep yourself calm, but you didn't listen."

"She was all over you, Micah," I defend.

"Yeah. She's good at that." He nods. "And you should have been good at trusting me."

"Trust you?" I fist my own hands and put them on my hips. "You're going to marry me tomorrow, Micah, because your father and my father deemed it so. Not because you love me—you don't even like me—and not because either of us want it. How can I trust you? You didn't even fight to allow my family here tonight. You let your father do this, let him try to humiliate me."

"Do you want me to love you?"

"What?" I'm caught off guard with the question. Do I? "No," I answer, moving my eyes from his. If he stares too hard at me, he'll see the truth. Feelings for him have crept into my heart. Not love, never that, but a warmth that feels like it's being chilled with this entire situation.

His lips kick up to the side in a playful grin. "I'll let you hold on to that for now."

"We aren't talking about that right now, Micah. Neither of us expect a romantic relationship. That's has nothing to do with what's happening." I'm almost convincing, except the dull ache builds in my chest again.

"You're right," he agrees. "Right now, we're talking about you acting like the spoiled princess my father thinks you are. I told you to behave." His hands move to his belt buckle and I'm shocked into silence as he pulls the leather from the metal buckle then zips it through the loops of his pants.

My ass clenches.

"So, you're going to be a good little boy and do your father's bidding, to deal with me?" Having the bed between us is lending me bravado.

He huffs a laugh as he concentrates on folding the belt in half and tucking the buckle into the palm of his hand.

"My father's way of dealing with women is drastically different than mine, Lena." After hearing the women in the stable crying, I don't doubt him. Roman is an evil man. Micah may be dangerous, and he may sometimes be cruel, but his heart isn't as black as I assumed.

"You think this is less humiliating? Everyone downstairs will know what you did." Tears prick my eyes. This is my own doing. He warned me. Even at the table, he warned me, but my temper flared, propped up by my pride.

"Everyone downstairs will assume whatever they want to assume no matter what happens right now, Lena." While holding the belt in his hand, he works the buttons open on his cuffs and works them into neat folds up to his elbows.

"Don't do this," I whisper. How much embarrassment am I to endure?

"Do you think you don't deserve a punishment?" He pauses in his folding.

I open my mouth, fully intending to deny I deserve anything, but the sound doesn't carry forth from my throat.

"I made it very clear what would happen if you behaved badly, didn't I?"

Not in exact words, but I can't deny that I understood what would happen.

"Micah." I say his name as though it will somehow take on a magical spell and convince him to give up his thoughts of taking that belt to my ass.

"Lena." He sighs. "I'm not fighting with you. Now, get out of that dress and bend over the bed."

I blink back the tears threatening and shove my chin up an inch.

"I won't."

"You won't?" His eyebrows raise, but there's a hint of joy in his eyes.

"Don't make me do this."

My last plea triggers something in him, and he rounds the bed in a flash. Before I blink, he's got his hand fisted in my hair and is walking me back away from the bed.

"Make you do this?" He drags me to the settee, spinning me away from him while keeping his hand fixated at my scalp. He grabs the neckline of the dress in the back and rips it downward until the material tears. Pink fabric and lace fall to my feet, beading rolls across the floor.

"Micah!" I twist hard, but only achieve in pulling my own hair.

In one more yank, he tears my panties from my ass.

"No." I pull, but nothing gets him to drop his hand. I'm shoved over the settee in the next movement and only then does his hand move from my hair. It's back on me between my shoulders, pinning me down.

The belt buckle jangles behind me, but it's only a second before the first fire-hot lash lands across my cheeks. I freeze, my body shocked at the immense sting spreading across my flesh. Another lash and then another. He's five swats in before he pauses.

"Who was rude at the dinner table tonight, Lena? Me or you?"

I suck in a harsh breath. Tears roll down my cheeks; this is so much worse than the hand spanking he gave me the first time. And it's nothing like the spanking he gave me only a few nights ago.

"Who?" He pinches my right ass cheek.

"Me. But—"

"No excuses. You let them get the better of you, and who won, Lena? You got in a good shot toward my father, toward Katina, but who's up here getting her ass blistered?"

I fist my hands.

"Don't you dare reach back here. I'll tie you down and give you twice the belting. You won't be sitting at your own fucking wedding."

The belt crashes down on me again, and I rise up to my toes. It doesn't help, nothing I do makes it easier for me or harder for him. The leather strap comes down again and again.

I sag over the settee. After another sharp lash, he drops the belt beside me.

"You're not being fair," I whisper, dragging in a shaky breath and trying to get myself composed.

"There is no fair in our world, princess. You know that."

"You want me to roll over and let them abuse me." I crane my neck, looking at him over my shoulder. "I'll never do that. Never."

His jaw tightens, but the sharpness of his eyes softens.

"You won't have to do that. I won't allow them to hurt you, and if you had kept your temper in check for another moment, I could have handled them. Instead, you took matters into your own hands and now we're here." He smacks my ass again, but only half-heartedly.

"I didn't know that," I admit.

"Was I unclear before?"

I turn back away from him. He's not angry about what I said, he's upset because I didn't trust him enough to let him deal with his father. Me stepping on Roman's toes caused more trouble than if Micah had done it. I made Micah look weak in the eyes of his men.

"I'm sorry," I say softly. "I thought you wanted Katina, that you wanted me to see that you'll be keeping her, and I would just have to watch."

He releases the pressure on my back and sits beside me, running his hand up and down my spine.

"I will never do that to you." He brushes away a stray hair that's stuck to my wet face. "I promise, Lena. I would never do that to you. Once I make my vows, I'll keep them."

A weight lifts from me with his proclamation. And I'm more confused than ever.

"Come here," he says as he lifts me from my position and pulls me into his lap. His pants are rough against the tenderness of my ass.

"I'm sorry that I embarrassed you or made you look bad, but I'm not sorry I upset your father," I confess once I'm settled on his lap.

He breaks into a laugh. "What am I going to do with you, princess?"

I shrug. "I suppose letting me out of all this is out of the question?"

He knuckles my chin toward him. There's a seriousness in his eyes, a stern set of his features.

"I'll never let you go, Lena. And not because of my father's orders." He kisses me, soft at first, then hard and possessive. Everything inside me comes alive. I'm left wanting when he pulls away.

"I'll never let you go, because I don't want to. You're mine, princess. Like it or not, you belong to me." He wipes his thumb across my cheek, clearing away the streaks of tears. Hopefully, my mascara has held up and I don't look as lousy as I feel.

"And Katina?" I ask, lowering my gaze. I shouldn't feel this level of jealousy, but it's nagging me nonetheless.

"She's the past and that's where she stays. You have to promise me not to let my father get you riled up. You only let him win when you lash out."

He's right. It felt good, seeing his cheeks turn red, hearing the surprised gasps of the guests, but in the end I lost.

"I'll try." It's the best I can do.

He sighs. "Try a lot, unless you'd like to have more evenings draped over the couch instead of beneath me in bed."

It's my turn to frown. "So... no reward?"

He laughs. "You're lucky I'm not making you go back downstairs."

I jump off his lap, ready to lock myself in the bathroom to avoid being dragged off.

"I said I wasn't making you." He stands from the couch. "I do have to go back down though. I need to talk with Niko before he takes off and I'm sure my father has a few words for me as well. You'll be going to bed."

"Going to bed, like some bad little girl," I scoff, grabbing my panties from the floor.

He snags the panties from me.

"Yes, because that's exactly how you behaved. To bed early with no dinner. Sounds like a just punishment." He smiles, and pockets my panties.

"I'm not going to be able to sleep. It's early."

He kisses my cheek and pats my still tender ass.

"Don't leave this room."

I can work with that. "I won't."

He stares at me a long moment. "It's going to be a very interesting day tomorrow."

"I'll be good."

He laughs as he collects his jacket and begins rolling down his sleeves.

"I've heard that before. Good night, princess." A quick peck to my cheek, and he's gone, closing the door to the bedroom behind him.

I glance down at the belt coiled up on the settee. Apparently, I'm going to have a love-hate relationship with more than Micah.

CHAPTER 19

$\mathcal{L}$ena

It's my wedding day. My hair's been pulled, twisted, and pinned into a glorious updo that I never would have pulled off without a professional. The makeup artist has finally finished packing up and left me alone. I've even been stuffed into the dress, thanks to Kasia's help.

And now, I'm standing in front of the full-length mirror on the inside of the closet trying to catch my breath. My family is here already. Kasia promised me Dominik and Jakub were keeping my father away from the Ivanovs.

"I think they'll be ready for you in a few minutes," Kasia says as she breezes back into the room.

I flatten my hand against my stomach and give a little nod. Slow breath in, one, two, three. Long breath out.

My nerves are everywhere, and nothing is working to keep them under control.

What if Roman says something to piss me off? What if Katina does? I don't want to ruin today.

"Hey, you okay?" Kasia steps behind me in the mirror. She's dressed in a simple purple dress with lilac ribbons braided into her long blonde hair.

"I'm fine," I say, closing my eyes. "I'm fine."

"Maybe you should sit."

"No." I shake my head. "I'm fine." I take another slow breath in, but my eyes fill with tears. I'm losing this battle and I'm going to destroy all the hard work that annoying makeup artist did.

"Lena." Kasia lightly grasps my arms and squeezes. "I know you're scared." She laughs softly. "I know better than anyone."

I blow out another long breath, gathering the ends of my frayed nerves and bundling them back together. When I turn to face her, the tears have receded and I'm able to stand firm.

"The difference is you were marrying my brother, not the son of the Ivanov family."

She tilts her head with narrowed eyes. "Do you think they are so different? Micah and Dominik?"

"My father doesn't keep an underground bunker full of women to be bought and sold like cattle."

"No. But he isn't an innocent man either. I don't know the full extent of what the Staszek family does, but I know Dominik gets calls in the middle of the night that drag him from bed. And when he returns, he's tense and worn out. More than once he's come home with blood on his clothes."

"Does he know you think so lowly of his family?" I ask, but the bitterness isn't real. She's right, there's little difference between my father and Roman. But my father is mine, and he would never hurt me. Roman would gladly see me thrown to the wolves.

"I don't think badly of your father or either of your brothers. This is the world we live in. If Dominik were to magically be on the outside of it, things wouldn't change. It wouldn't take the drugs off the streets."

"Roman's sins are different."

She nods. "They are. I agree." Reaching out, she straightens the thin strap over my shoulder. "You aren't powerless, Lena."

"I've never thought I was."

She grins. "I heard about last night's dinner."

I groan. "My humiliation?"

"No! You stood up for yourself. I'm sure Micah wasn't pleased, and I know Roman is still seething over it, but you didn't back down. You're nobody's footstool."

I roll my shoulders back. "You know when I was younger, Dominik complained to my father that he gave in to me too much. That he spoiled me."

She laughs. "I've heard that, yes."

"Dominik was too busy being Dad's first son to really pay attention. It wasn't that I had my dad wrapped around my finger, but that when I wanted something, truly wanted it, I just didn't give up until I got it."

"And is now different? You don't like what's happening, what can you do to change it?"

"Do you need any help at the shelter? I can't offer much but my time."

She breaks into a bright smile. "That would be great."

"Seems such a small act compared to the horrors I know Roman is causing."

Kasia's smile slips a fraction. "We do what we can. Who knows, maybe one day we'll have the force to make him shut it down."

"And until then? I'll still be an Ivanov."

She grasps my hands tightly. "And you'll still be you."

"Hey, you guys done messing around? They're waiting for you down there." Jakub bursts into the room. For a brief moment he reminds me of when we were children and Dad would send him up to fetch me for dinner. Half annoyed at being given the task.

"Yeah. I'm ready." I take another deep breath.

"Sorry. My fault." Kasia waves at him. "I'll run ahead and sit with Dominik." She wiggles her fingers at me and disappears.

Jakub takes a long look at me; his annoyance slips to concern.

"You're marrying Micah Ivanov," he says, as though it's the first time he's allowed himself to say the words out loud. "If he ever hurts you, Lena—"

"Oh, spare me the big brother speech, Jakub." I wave at him and go in search of the floral bouquet I'm meant to use for the ceremony.

His jaw clenches. "I've been busy with the club, with my own shit. If I'd been paying more attention, maybe I could have saved you from this."

I meet him at the door, flowers in hand. "I'm not being taken to the executioner, Jakub. Just the altar."

His frown deepens. "Dad's married off Dominik, and now you. I suppose I'll be next."

I laugh. "Just like you to think of yourself."

He breaks into a grin. "Can't help it. I'm not ready to be tied down."

I lightly smack his shoulder. "Let's get this over with. I want to get out of Roman's house and that won't happen until I have Micah's ring on my finger."

He nods and loops his arm through mine.

"I am serious, Lena," he says as we teeter at the top of the stairs. My father stands at the bottom waiting for us. Music plays behind him. "If he hurts you. You come home. You call me. You call Dominik. You get away from him."

I squeeze my brother's arm. "I can take care of myself, Jakub."

He opens his mouth like he's going to say something else, but then snaps his lips closed.

"Yes, you can, little sister." He points at the stairs. "Are you ready?"

My stomach twists, but as we take the first step down a gentle calm rushes over me and by the time we meet my father I'm solid in my steps.

"Lena." My father takes me from Jakub. "I know I haven't been available since—"

"It's all right, Daddy." I slip my arm through his. "I'm all right."

I have to say it again quietly in my mind as he leads me to the back patio where I'm greeted with a small crowd. Music plays, the guests stand, and my father pulls me toward the aisle.

Then I catch Micah's stare.

Everything will be all right.

It has to be.

CHAPTER 20

M*icah*

My wife stands with her brothers and her sister-in-law while I speak with Niko and Dimitri. We aren't staying long after the meal is served, and I want them ready.

When Lena glided down the rolled-out white carpet, tucked into her father's side, my heart threatened to jump out of my chest. It wasn't just her beauty—and fuck was she beautiful with her hair pinned up and the large curls pouring out framing her face, and that dress. Holy hell, it shouldn't be legal for a woman to walk around with such generous curves and regal appearance. With each step she took, her confidence glowed around her. It was in those moments her beauty outshined any other woman before her.

"Be ready to go right after we eat. I don't want to spend another minute here than I have to," I say and head toward where my wife huddles with her family.

Before I can get to her, Roman stops me. "Remember what I told you."

I meet his gaze. The man is obsessed, and it's starting to show in other areas of the business. Niko had a report for me this morning that has me on edge. Roman's pouring more capital into the stable than we can cover with legitimate investments. He's going to get us all in trouble. A war with another family can be dealt with. But a full-out war with the feds can easily break us apart. Especially if he's bankrupted the family with his pet project.

"I got it," I assure him and press forward. The sooner I get Lena away from him, the better for us all.

Katina stands off to the corner of the patio, talking with one of my cousins. She catches my stare and smiles but makes no move to engage me. Other than when she's forced, she's harmless. And she has no true interest in me, not that she would get anywhere if she did.

I meant what I told Lena.

I may not have come to this marriage of my own free will, but I will not go back on my vows. I will not betray her.

"Lena." I touch her elbow. "Dominik, Jakub." I nod toward her brothers. "Kasia."

Lena stiffens beneath my touch, but she holds herself strong. She's been so good today for me. Other than mild complaints about the hairdresser and makeup artist, she has done everything asked of her quietly. I don't mistake her obedience here as weakness; no, my princess has claws and she's willing to use them when needed.

It's only one of the many things I'm starting to understand and admire about her.

"I'm sorry to tear you away, but I need to see you for a minute." I tug on her elbow.

"Of course." She hands her glass of wine to Kasia. "I'll be right back."

Dominik's glare is steadfast, but I can't blame him. If the roles were reversed, I'm not sure I'd behave as well as they have. I'm sure he fantasizes about sticking a knife in my heart, but he won't mess up this truce. We have that in common.

"What do you need?" Lena asks as I lead her through the house toward the stairs.

"I need you upstairs for a minute," I say and bring her up the stairs to our room.

"Micah. People will notice we've gone missing," she says as we come to our suite.

I smile at her, enjoying the way her pupils dilate with the mere thought of us being alone in the bedroom.

"Do you think I give a fuck about that?" I ask, pushing the door open and motioning for her to get inside.

She sighs. "I guess not."

I follow her in then lock the door behind her. While she stands in the middle of the sitting room watching me, I go into the bedroom and retrieve what I'm looking for from my bag and return to her.

Her eyes land on the item in my hand and her cheeks explode into a blush.

"Micah, what are you thinking to do?" Her hands fly behind her, as though she could actually block me from my intent.

"I told you, princess. On our wedding night, I'll take the one virginity you still have." I open my hand and let the silver bullet-shaped plug stand in my palm. "This makes it easier for you later."

Her jaw slacks, her pretty lips part, then snap shut again.

"Speechless? Well, now I know how to achieve that," I laugh. It's easy, this bit of banter between us. Even with her embarrassment and arousal mingling, the tension eases comfortably.

"You can't think to actually use that thing right now." She moves back a step. "We're expected at the luncheon."

I advance toward her. "I know."

"You're out of your mind. I'm not doing that." She folds her arms over her chest.

"Lena, look at me," I order when she keeps her pitiful gaze fixated on my chest.

Her attention eases its way up to me.

"Do you remember your vows?"

Her brows wrinkle. "What?"

"The vows, the ones you just took barely an hour ago before God and our family?" I remind her.

"There was nothing about butt plugs in them."

I hold back my chuckle. This woman can make nearly any situation lighter with her quick wit. It will definitely be her undoing some days. I look forward to them.

"What were they, Lena? You promised to…" I wave my hand at her to fill in the blanks.

She sighs.

"To love, honor, and—" She stops, scrunching up her nose. "Obey."

"Obey. Yes." I snap my fingers. "That's the one we're focusing on now. So, you can either obey me, *wife*, or you can earn a spanking, then have the plug put in anyway. And this time, I won't go lightly with my belt."

Her lips squish together. Whatever internal battle she's having, I'm not sure she's going to come out the winner.

"Fine." She marches at me and snatches the plug from my hand and turns toward the other bedroom. I grab her arm before she gets two steps away.

"Where are you going?"

"To put this damn thing in," she snaps.

"Nope. Not that easy, princess." I pluck the plug from her grasp and pull her into the bedroom we shared last night.

"It will take me ten minutes to get out of this thing," she complains.

"You don't need to, just bend over the edge of the bed and lift up the dress." I look over the gown; it's elegant, not full of tooling and lace, but sleek and beautiful. Like her.

While I retrieve a small bottle of lubrication, she gets situated over the side of the bed. Her dislike for what's about to happen makes her look more like a child being made to take her vitamins than a woman about to submit willingly to her husband.

I can fix that.

As I grab the lube, I pick up the small vibrator I packed in the hopes we were going to have fun last night. But thanks to her outburst, that hadn't happened.

I sit on the bed beside her upturned ass. Sadly, there aren't any marks from yesterday. She's already pulled her white lace panties down to her knees and buried her face in the bed.

"It's not as bad as you think."

"Just do it," she mutters into the bedding.

"Reach back here and pull your ass apart for me. Show me your dark little hole." My cock lengthens at my own words.

She groans but does my bidding.

"I think I have something that will make this better for you," I say, twisting the bottom of the vibrator on and slipping it between her legs. There's enough pressure of her body against the bed to hold it in place, right on her clit.

"Oh!" She sinks into the sensations.

"Better?"

Her nails turn inward, clenching her cheeks. It's enough of an answer.

I squirt a dollop of lubrication on the dark ring of muscle. Instantly she clenches.

"Nope. If you do that, I have to take the vibrator away," I warn as I drop the lubrication bottle behind me on the bed.

Slowly, she eases.

"Feel good?" I ask, tapping the end of the vibrator. "Keep focused on how good it feels while I'm inserting the plug."

"I can't believe I'm letting you do this," she mutters, and I'm sure I'm not supposed to hear it.

The rounded edge of the plug is poised at her asshole.

"Should you do it and I'll watch?" I ask, half threatening. She's never had this done and I'm not sure I want to give up the pleasure of being the one to handle it for her.

She twists her head enough to look at me with her wide eyes. "No, you do it."

I pat her ass with my free hand. "That's a good princess," I tease her and it's enough to get her body to relax. When she moves her focus from what I'm doing, it won't be so hard to get the plug in place.

"Deep breath, baby," I say softly over the hum of the vibrator. It's doing its job of making her pussy nice and wet. Her lips glisten with her juices. It's a shame she isn't going to find any relief until I have her in our bed tonight.

I push gingerly at first, watching the tight muscles stretch around the plug, more and more as it gets to the widest part of the toy.

"It burns," she whines.

"Push out at me, Lena. It will relax the muscle more."

"I can't do that."

"Your choice. Either way it's going in." I push it more and she hisses. It only takes her another breath to finally get in line with what I want from her. Her asshole swallows up the rest of the plug and tightens around the thin base. The lavender jewel at the base is the only bit of it visible now.

I smile at the sweetness of it. Of her. I snag the vibrator.

"You can let go now." I stand up from the bed, watching as her cheeks fall back into place and hug the jeweled end of her plug. I adjust my rock-hard cock in my pants. After I pocket the vibrator, I pull her panties up over her creamy, lush ass.

I grab the lube and take it, along with the vibe, to my bag and toss them inside. When I turn back around, she stands beside the bed, every inch of her face covered in a deep crimson blush. She tries to cover her embarrassment by fixing the skirt of her dress.

"Come here, princess." I crook my finger at her. Fire bursts into her eyes.

"What now?" she demands while she makes her way over to me.

"You'll be good at lunch. No matter what." I press my finger to her lips just as they start to move. "I will deal with anything my father throws at us. I'm asking you to trust me here, Lena. Trust that I will take care of you."

"I can take care of myself," she says against my finger.

I drop my hand to her cheek, running the back of my fingers along her jaw.

"I know you can, which makes it all the more meaningful when you put your safety into my hands." I cup the back of her neck and pull her to me, capturing her mouth beneath mine. The kiss at the altar had been quick, but not this one.

I wrap my second hand around her throat, trapping her neatly in place as I deepen the kiss. Her throat vibrates beneath my palm when I squeeze—not enough to cut off her air, only enough to let her feel me, truly feel me.

When I break the kiss, I hold her throat tighter.

"I will always keep you safe, Lena."

She lays her hands on my chest with no pressure. Her chin moves up to accommodate my large hand, but she doesn't resist. When her pupils are fully dilated, I let her go.

"Can you do that for me? Can you trust me today?" It's a small step in the right direction.

She trails her fingertips along her throat, where the last bit of my fingerprints fades.

"Yes, Micah. I think I can."

CHAPTER 21

ena

"Something wrong?" Micah asks me as we stand silently in the elevator taking us up to his penthouse. Our penthouse. We're married now; I guess that means it's my home, too.

"No." I keep my eyes fixated on the lighted numbers as they flash.

"You keep wiggling. Are your pants too tight?" he asks, slinking his arm around my waist and pulling me closer to him. He's enjoying this an annoying amount.

"They're fine." But they aren't. When I packed a pair of slacks to wear after the luncheon, I hadn't been aware of his intention to stick a damn plug up my ass. Now I'm wearing a pair of snugly fitting ivory slacks with an off the shoulder tan knit sweater. The slacks hug me enough to remind me of the plug with every move.

I'm not sure how I made it through the luncheon with this thing inside me. Or how I was able to carry on a conversation with anyone while my pussy soaked through my panties because I could feel the heat of Micah's stare whenever he turned in my direction. He knew I had this thing lodged in my ass. With that knowledge, coupled with the ripples of arousal spreading through my core with my movements, I was a puddle of need.

"You and Kasia had a lot to talk about," he says, switching topics just as he punches in the code to open the doors.

"She's actually really nice." I step inside.

"The conversation looked serious."

"It was," I say, following him from the foyer to the kitchen. He grabs a bottle of wine and two glasses.

"Are you hoping I won't find out what you're up to?" he asks while uncorking the bottle and pouring each of us a glass of red wine.

I take my glass and press my hip against the counter. He's going to find out. It's not like I'll be able to hide anything I do from this man. He'll always have eyes on me.

"I'm going to be volunteering at Kasia's halfway house." I swirl the wine around the glass then take a casual sip.

He puts his glass down on the counter. "My father doesn't want you seeing your family for the time being." He stops my reaction with a hand in the air. "I'm not telling you to stay away from them. I'll deal with my father, but I need you to give me some time."

"Are you saying I can't see Kasia? Jakub? My father?"

He stares at me a long moment. "No." He shakes his head and slides around the kitchen island until he's next to me and picks up my hand. "I'm saying I need you to be cautious. Don't do anything that makes him think you're acting against our family."

"How is helping clean up rooms and doing laundry going to be interpreted that way?"

He half smiles. "My father has an active imagination. That place helps rescue women from men like him. He'll see it as an act against us. So, just let me deal with him first before you start going there."

"Trust you." I repeat his earlier words.

He brings my hand to his lips. "Yes, Lena. Trust me."

"How long? I told Kasia I'd be over in a few days."

He turns my hand until my palm faces up. His tongue skates across my wrist before he kisses the spot.

"A day or two," he says, kissing my palm. If he's trying to distract me, it's working.

"And then you won't get in the way?"

He looks up from my hand, his forehead wrinkled, his eyes dark and focused. "Get in your way?" He laughs and lets my hand go. "You talk big."

"I'm only clarifying that once you calm your father, you'll let me go about my life. I don't want to spend the rest of my life waiting for permission for ordinary things." And I won't, but I'm sure he knows that about me by now.

"Oh, I'll always keep an eye on you," he promises with a sultry smile. "Trust me, Lena. Things can be very good between us. We aren't enemies." His fingertips skate across my jaw. "And I don't want to talk about our families right now."

"Oh? What would you like to talk about then?"

He leans in and captures my mouth beneath his. The warm tingle ramps up into a full explosion when his hand moves around me and he presses against the plug.

"I don't want any talking at all." He pushes my wineglass away. Apparently, the small talk is over. "Get in the bedroom, princess, and get out of this outfit." He plucks the neckline of my sweater.

I keep my head held high as I march to the bedroom. His hot stare beats on the back of me as he follows behind. The click of his shoes against the flooring mimics the harsh beat of my heart as we get closer and closer to our room with each step.

Once inside the sitting room, I pause. He's not willing to give me time to overthink things, though, and grabs my hand in his, pulling me to the bedroom.

"Micah." I yank free of his grip once I'm faced with the bed and what I have in store for me. The plug was one thing, but to have his cock buried deep within me is another.

"I told you to get out of those clothes, Lena," he says as his response to my quiet plea. After leaving me standing at the foot of the bed, he shakes out of his jacket. His tie easily glides out from beneath his collar and he tosses it onto the nightstand. He toes out of his shoes and unbuttons his shirt.

"Do you need a reminder of your vows again?" he asks me when he reaches to undo his belt, and I'm still standing frozen in time.

The image of having that leather belt slapping across my cheeks with the plug firmly in place gets me moving.

Once I'm completely nude, I look back at him. My nipples harden beneath his predatory gaze. He's removed his shirt but left his pants on. While avoiding his eyes, I let my own wander over his body. He's sculpted and trim.

"Lena." He says my name sharply and I meet his gaze again. "Lie on the bed." He points where he wants me. I must have missed his first order.

I climb on the bed, lying back on the oversized soft pillows. I wonder if I could press one over my face until this ordeal was over.

The bed dips as he climbs on with me.

"I'm not going to kill you, for fuck's sake, Lena. Relax." He grabs my knees and shoves my thighs apart. The cool air of the room brushes across my wet sex.

"Look at me, princess," he orders with less tension. He's impatient, but he's not angry. "Relax for me."

He scoots himself down on the bed until his face hovers over my pussy.

"I've wanted to do this since I met you," he says darkly as his head dips lower. His hot breath washes over my pussy lips, over my swollen and wanting clit. I fist my hands, digging my nails into my palms.

If I don't distract myself, I'll beg him to hurry. I've wanted his mouth on me for ages it seems.

His tongue skates up and down my folds. Using his thumbs, he spreads my lips open to expose my clit to his attentions. I close my eyes and suppress a cry of arousal when the tip of his tongue lavishes ecstasy across my clit.

"Fuck, princess," he groans, sweeping his tongue through my slit, up and down, then flicking across the most sensitive part of my bud.

"Micah!" I tense as the flood of arousal builds behind a dam I can't hold back for much longer.

"Not yet, princess." He laughs, then slides two fingers into my pussy. Turning his hand, he presses downward into my passage, hard and fast as his mouth envelops my clit.

"Fuck!" I yell out, arching from the bed as wave after wave crashes over my body. "Micah. Micah!" I scream, uncaring of anything other than the explicit heaven raining down over my body as I come.

I wind my fingers into his short dark hair, arching my hips against his mouth. He never stops licking and biting as the orgasm ebbs and I'm left a puddle in the center of our bed. He places another kiss to my clit, then sits up on his heels.

A heated flush rushes over my body with him staring down at me like he's just caught me with my hand in a cookie jar.

"Did I say you could come, Lena?" he asks with a hint of danger on the edge.

"You didn't say I couldn't," I reply, easing my knees closed. He stops me quickly by shoving them back to the mattress and canvassing my inner thighs with harsh slaps.

"Such a mouthy wife." He tsks his tongue then reaches between my legs again, tapping his finger to the plug. "Take a deep breath, Lena."

I barely have time to compose myself before he pulls the plug out, stretching me further with the wide part of it as he does so. Once it's out, he tosses it to the floor.

I'm stuck lying on the bed, my legs spread out exposed to him—ready for the fucking he's promised me as he works his pants and boxers off.

When his cock is free, it bobs toward me, thick and long. And it's going in my ass. I clench my fists again.

Micah blankets my body with his own, trailing kisses up my jaw until he reaches my mouth. Once his lips touch mine, I'm lost to him again. Arousal swirls alive within me. The thick head of his cock presses against my wet passage.

When I wiggle my hips, wanting to fill myself with his cock, he breaks the kiss. "No, no, I'm fucking your tight virgin ass tonight, Lena."

He reaches between our bodies and fists his cock, gathering up the juices of my pussy on the tip before pressing it against my asshole. Instinct kicks in and I clench.

"Keep doing that and this won't be any fun for you," he warns, pushing forward still, undeterred by my nervousness.

"Micah. I don't think... shouldn't we use the plug more first? Maybe do this... oh!" I grab his shoulders as he thrusts forward, breaking through my ring of muscle.

"See, not so bad." He grits his teeth, as though he's the one having trouble keeping himself composed. "How does that feel?"

"Full." I stiffen as he shifts again.

"You're going to take it; every inch of my cock is going to plow into your ass and you're going to accept it."

His crass words only work to drive my arousal to a higher peak.

"Yes, Micah." I nod, running my hands over his bare shoulders. Having him so close to me like this, so intimately against me, calms me. He won't hurt me. Not in any permanent way. "I trust you," I say.

It's like I've turned the key on the engine with my words. His eyes roll back, and he pushes forward, fully embedding his thick cock into my ass. I cry out at the sudden invasion, but he gives me no time to acclimate to his size.

Harder and faster, he plows his cock into my ass and all I can do is take what he gives me. What starts out as sharp bits of pain quickly turns into fragments of need, embers of want, and erupts into a volcanic proportion of desire.

"Don't stop," I plead when he slows. My words trigger a seductive, devilish grin from him, and he moves forward again.

"You like my cock in your ass, princess."

"Harder, Micah!" I demand and spread my legs further.

"Your clit, bossy girl, rub your clit."

I slide my hand between our bodies as he continues to fuck my ass. As soon as my fingertip grazes my clit, fireworks threaten inside.

The sounds of flesh slapping flesh dance over our bodies as he wraps his arms beneath me. He snakes his hands around my shoulders, pulling me toward him as he thrusts forward into me. Every fiber of my body is on high alert.

He plows forward hard enough to bounce the headboard off the wall, but it's not enough. I want more, I want everything he can give me. The stretch, the fullness, it all lifts me into an aroused state of panic. Rubbing my clit frantically, I chase down the impossible.

Another thrust from him, and it happens. Vibrant colors cascade behind my eyelids. I thrust my hips up at him, matching his fevered strokes, riding the waves of pleasure as heated spasms course through me.

A low growl rumbles from deep within him and his pumping increases. Another thrust and another, then he stills with a roar of release. Thick ropes of hot cum spurt inside my ass, filling me with his seed.

Our breath, hot and heavy, mingles between us just before he presses his lips to mine. His forehead falls to mine, just before he pulls back, his cock slips from my ass and he slinks to lie beside me.

"Micah," I say when moments pass quietly. "I need a towel, or something." This never gets less awkward, I think. The messiness of afterwards.

He rolls to his side and leans up on his elbow. His hair is disheveled, and a loose black lock of hair falls over his eye. It's enough to make me wet for him all over again.

"Never wipe my cum from you." He reaches down to my legs and pulls them closed. "I want you to feel me dripping down between your ass cheeks, down your thighs, and remember who you belong to."

I blink up at him, suddenly hot beneath my own skin. The mark of ownership—that's what he's getting at, and I don't hate it.

"Can I at least get under the blanket?" I ask, forcing attitude into my words.

He grins and shifts back so I can maneuver the blankets and get beneath them. There's going to be a mess on the sheets in the morning, but something tells me he'll only be more proud of himself for it.

Micah climbs beneath the covers with me. His heavy arm pulls me closer to his body. The late afternoon sun rays peek through the blinds, casting the room in an orange glow.

"It's too early to go to bed," I say just as a large yawn takes over.

He hugs me tighter to him. "Who said you're going to bed." He kisses the back of my shoulder. "You can have a nap, but then I'm fucking you again."

Since he's behind me and can't see me, I grin at the prospect.

"And again."

I laugh then snuggle into the pillows and press myself into the comfort of his embrace. A short nap will do me good.

Could this be reality? Will things settle into this sort of calm that I can rely on?

I grab onto the first signs of sleep. If it's only a dream for this moment, I'll happily fall into it.

CHAPTER 22

 icah

I find my father in his office in the back of the house. This last week with Lena has put a rose-colored shade over the reality of my work. But it's time I get back into the full swing of things with the Ivanov business.

As I enter Roman's office a young woman, much younger than Lena, slithers past me. One of Roman's men steps out to greet her and grabs her arm, half dragging her away from the office.

"Ah. Micah." Roman zips up his pants and tucks his shirt back in. "I almost forgot you were coming today. It's been so long since I've seen you."

I watch the girl being pulled down a corridor that leads to the underground entrance to the stable. It wasn't that long ago I walked through that very hallway to speak with Lena.

After I shut the office door, I shake off the memory of her being kept in that rancid place. Rats are treated better than those women.

"I've been busy with the restaurant and the clubs." I hand him a folder with all the bookkeeper reports. "We're pulling in a much larger profit than I thought we would the first year." I point at the folder.

He drops it to his desk without opening it and heads to his bar to make himself a drink.

"And all that profit will disappear once the taxman comes to collect." He rolls his head from one shoulder to the other. "But it's a good way to keep the feds off our asses." He tips his glass back and downs his drink.

"I've put in a bid on a property in Skokie and another out in Naperville. If both go our way, we'll be expanding the restaurant." I slide my hands into my pockets. It's a bold move to expand so quickly, but right now we have a waitlist of several months. Moving to the right suburbs will spread the word. I didn't invest so much money in this venture to see it fail. It will succeed.

"So soon?"

"It gives us room to grow all aspects of the business," I explain. I have every intention of bringing more legal businesses into the fold, but I can't deny the profits we gain with the avenues we walk on the other side of the law.

His eyebrows arch. "Ah, I see. Explain."

"The more legal businesses we have, the more we can run through the business."

He thinks for a moment. "That's true. We can wash our own laundry instead of depending on so many outsiders."

"Yes."

"Okay, then. Good. That's good thinking, Micah." He points at me. "And the stable? Have you given thought on how to best expand the operation?"

I roll my shoulders back. "Yes. I've been thinking about it, and I'm not sure expanding that part of the business is a good idea right now."

What little light had bloomed in his eyes at my idea to expand the restaurants diminishes. "I told you what I have planned."

"I know." I keep my tone level; any provocation and he'll throw up his brick wall of ignorance. "I've been going over those numbers as well, looking at everything that goes into it and I'm not sure doubling it is a good idea right now. It's not as profitable as the other streams of income we have; doubling down on it could put us in the red."

"You question me?" His accusation comes at me hard, coupled with the same dark disapproval he's had for me over the years. After Igor's death it only grew.

"No, I'm questioning the numbers, the projections," I point out. Money, he understands. It's probably the only thing he understands.

"Money will be made." He pours another drink. "We can lower our costs. Sell more. It will work."

"The costs will double if you take in more than you already do. And where will you house between shipments?"

He huffs. "Double up in the cells. It will be fine."

"There's no reason to double. Why are you so insistent on this part of the business? It's not making the family as much money as our other streams. There's no reason—"

"Your brother never would have spoken to me like this," he seethes at me. "Igor knew this business, he built it and you want to tear it down!"

"Tear it down? No. But don't double down on something that's not going to double profits. It's basic math."

His eyes narrow to slits. "This is that Polish slut getting into your head."

I move my hands from my pockets and take a step in his direction. "My wife's name is Lena," I say with gritted teeth. "I won't have you talking like that about her."

His brows shoot up. "Oh? You're going to tell me how to talk now?"

"She's my wife."

"Because I made it so. She's supposed to be used to humiliate that fucking family, but instead you have her living like a fucking princess up in your tower!" Spittle flies from his mouth. "She's going to be volunteering at that whorehouse of her brothers'?"

"You don't need to have your men talk behind my back, you can just ask me, and I'll be happy to tell you everything I'm doing," I shoot back at him. "She's volunteering at the halfway house, yes. And no, she won't be used in your little game of revenge. What is your obsession?" I ask again, having had enough of secrets and backroom conversations.

He stares at me for a long moment.

"You're more like your brother than I thought," he says, but it's not a compliment. I've never heard him sound so sour when it came to Igor.

"Igor would agree with me. The stable isn't worth more investment." I stand my ground, knowing I'm on thin ice.

"He probably would." He nods. "Your brother let his fucking cock lead him away from family loyalty, too. Just like you."

"What does that mean?"

His lips curl inward. A deep red splatters over his cheeks. I'm not sure if he's going to swing at me or pull his gun out and shoot me—his anger shakes the air between us.

"It means you both make me do things I don't want to do. When Igor failed, I had hoped you would succeed. But I see that's not going to happen."

"You aren't making any sense. Igor did nothing but exactly what you wanted."

"He betrayed me, just like you are."

"He didn't do anything to you." I fist my hands. Roman is off on a tangent; keeping him corralled to one subject will be hard now that he's let his temper get the best of him.

"No?" He slams his empty glass onto the bar. "Igor didn't understand the Staszek family was not our friends. That dirty Polish fucking family pulled him in."

"What are you talking about?"

"While you were off going to college and working so fucking hard getting your clubs and your restaurants up and running, your brother was befriending the fucking Staszek boy. And then he turned on our family, talking crazy shit about shutting down the stable. Not slowing down, but shutting down." He charges at me but stops short of running into me. "You both are fucking weak. I am ashamed to have my blood running through your fucking veins."

I stare at him in silence, letting his words sink in.

"Igor was friends with Dominik?" I ask.

"No. The other one, the young one." He wipes a hand across his mouth. "He let that Polish prick talk him into getting rid of the stable—all for some girl."

The pieces fall into place.

"Did you hurt Igor?" I demand, the idea popping out of my mouth before my brain filters it out.

He steps back as though I struck him.

"No," he yells. "I did no such thing." Pain breaks up the anger in his eyes, and I can't help but believe him. No matter what Igor did to piss him off, Roman loved him. But even though he didn't physically harm him, my father has ways of hurting people in worse ways.

My phone buzzes in my pocket. Probably Niko again. I'll deal with him later.

"My not wanting to expand the stables has nothing to do with Lena," I assure my father calmly. "It has everything to do with profits, and there won't be any if you chase after ventures that don't produce."

He keeps his glare in place and shakes his head. "You aren't in charge of this family yet, Micah. You'll do what you're told. The business lines are my domain, and until I'm cold in my grave, you'll keep doing what you're commanded to do."

My jaw aches, I clench so tightly. There's little I can do without fully insulting him, which would result in my wife being put in danger. Myself being put on a fucking stake.

"As long as you understand, Lena is not to be humiliated. She's my wife now, and any embarrassment she feels reflects on me. If you disrespect her, you disrespect me." I point at him. "You are my father, and the head of this family, but she is my responsibility. The day she put my ring on her finger is the day she became an Ivanov, and any action against her is an action against us all." He wants to throw around family loyalty, then we can both have ammunition in that fight.

"Perhaps you should go, Micah, before I do something we both regret." He moves to his desk and sinks into his chair, steeling his hands in front of him. "Go home. Think about where your loyalties lie."

I've been effectively dismissed.

On my way out of the house, my father's housekeeper, Katarina, tries to start up a conversation, but I dodge her. This house is no longer welcoming.

I have nothing here. And when I find out the truth of all the things he spewed at me, I doubt I will ever be returning.

CHAPTER 23

*L*ena

Micah is quiet in the car on the way to Katfish. He's been brooding ever since he returned from Roman's house this afternoon.

"You don't have to come if you have things to do," I say to him as the car pulls to a stop outside the club. "I'm sure my brothers can get me a ride home."

"No," he says and climbs out the car.

A moment later my door opens and his hand thrusts at me. I grab it and let him help me down from the SUV. As soon as the door shuts, Dimitri drives off, probably to find somewhere to park.

"Are you sure? You seem, I don't know, not here."

"I'm fine." Again, he's curt. We bypass the crowd waiting to get into the club and find our way to the VIP section in the back of the first floor.

Kasia and Dominik are already here, and Kasia gets up from the booth to hug me. Dominik and Micah nod in greeting but say nothing to each other.

Maybe I shouldn't have pushed him to come to Katfish. Just because he doesn't seem to have the same irrational hatred for my family as his father doesn't mean this isn't difficult for him. Especially since Roman had tried to keep me away from all of them.

Maybe that's the problem.

"Is your father angry at you for letting me see my family? Did he say something when you were there today?" I lean over to ask Micah so my brother can't hear me. The last thing I need is my overprotective brother getting involved.

He covers my hand on the table. "I don't want to talk about Roman tonight."

When I pull back to inspect his eyes, I see a familiar darkness.

"Yeah, okay." I nod.

"Where's Jakub?" Micah asks Dominik.

"In the office, he had an interview," Dominik answers, his jaw clenches.

"I need to speak with him." Micah gets up from the booth and gives me a quick look. "I'll be right back."

Before I can speak, he's gone.

"What's wrong with him?" Kasia asks.

I watch him maneuver through the crowd on the edge of the dance floor until he disappears into the sea of bodies.

"He saw his father this afternoon." I shrug.

"That's reason enough to put anyone in a bad mood," Kasia says with a smile.

"What did he meet with him about?" Dominik interjects, his eyes wandering over the room. I wonder if he ever rests enough not to notice every bit of action in his surroundings.

"He didn't say, but he hasn't seen him since the wedding so I'm sure Roman gave him grief over it."

"I'll be back. You two don't get in any trouble while I'm gone." Dominik kisses Kasia's cheek then gets up and leaves.

"What is he doing?"

Kasia shrugs. "He's probably going to eavesdrop on Jakub."

"He holds the reins too tightly on Jakub," I say.

"That's probably true. But enough about them, how are things with you?"

"As good as I would expect, I suppose."

Kasia laughs.

"What?" I demand.

"I saw the disappointment in you when Micah walked away. Things are going better than good, I'd say."

"He works a lot. Gets calls at all hours of the night." I shrug. Putting my feelings for Micah beneath a microscope is not what this evening is about. Micah needs a night out, a few hours where he's not working. Though I'm sure he only said yes to coming to Katfish so I could see my brothers.

"That won't change." Kasia's smile fades a bit at the edges. "It's just part of who they are. It doesn't mean anything about you if that's what you're worried about."

"I'm not worried." I straighten my shoulders. "I couldn't care less what Micah does. It's his life, he can do what he wants."

Kasia laughs again, harder this time. "Lena. You're not a very good liar."

"I'm not lying."

"Yes, you are, but you probably don't even know it yet. You like him. A lot, by the looks of things." Kasia reaches across the table and lays her hand on mine. "It's hard to understand falling in love with someone you were supposed to hate. It goes against logic, I know. Believe me." She squeezes my hand. "I know."

Love him?

I gear up to argue, to dispute everything she says, but there's a sense of calm that comes over me as I think on it. Am I falling in love with him?

"Don't worry too much over it. It's not like you have a choice in the matter. And besides, it wouldn't be the worst thing in the world to love your husband." Kasia pats my hand and sits back in her seat. "I wish Jakub would get a new DJ."

The music had switched over to a sharp techno beat that sounded like an assault on my eardrums.

I lean back in my seat. A waiter stops at our table and delivers Kasia and me a glass of wine that we didn't order. Dominik had it sent over, he tells us.

"When do your classes start?" Kasia sips at her fresh drink.

"Next week." I wrap my fingers around the stem of my glass. Micah's been gone a while and so has Dominik. The VIP section is less noisy than the rest of the club thanks to Jakub's installment of noise-dampening features, so it's easier to talk with Kasia, but still, a chill runs over me. Something isn't right.

"I'll be back in a minute." I slide my drink to the middle of the table and scoot from the table.

"No. Don't leave me here by myself." She follows me from the table. "Where are we going anyway?" she asks as we wiggle past a bachelorette party.

"To find Micah."

"He's probably not going to like that." She tugs on my arm. "So, let me go first. I'll say I was looking for Dominik."

I see no reason not to shelter behind her, so I let her get in front of me and let her lead the way toward the offices in the back.

The music fades as we make our way down the corridor to Jakub's office. Once we're at his door, tense voices creep from behind.

"It was a long time ago; I don't remember much," Jakub says. Kasia reaches for the handle, but I pull her hand away and shake my head at her.

Whatever conversation is happening inside, I want the organic version.

"But he spoke to you about my father's business." Micah's tense voice comes through clear.

"He mentioned he wished he hadn't helped build the damn stable. That's all, Micah. Look, I partied with him a few times. We weren't close. Most of what he said was while he was piss drunk."

"Why does any of this matter, anyway?" Dominik's voice chimes in.

"Roman sees it differently. He believes that you put the idea into his head about getting rid of the stables. He blames you for it," Micah explains.

My chest twists at the news. Roman idolized Igor from what Micah has told me. If he truly believes my family turned Igor from one of Roman's projects, that explains his taste for vengeance now. After Dominik stopped one of their shipments, it all exploded for Roman.

"It had nothing to do with me," Jakub insists, his tone turning angry. "Igor was involved with some girl. She was the reason."

"I think I know who you're talking about," Micah says, calmer now. "One second," he says and a few seconds later he says, "Niko. What?"

I look down at Kasia, who has crouched down trying to see through the blinds of the window beside the door. She turns a curious glance up at me. What do we do now? Just stay out here and eavesdrop or get in there and find out what exactly is going on?

"He was willing to sell?" Micah's voice starts up again. "How much... uh huh... two hundred fifty? That's all? What's her condition?"

A sharp tingle zips up my spine. He's buying a woman?

"Fine, yeah, that's good. Get the doctor to look her over."

I shove away from the door. "I've heard enough."

"Lena, wait." Kasia pulls at my arm. "Don't leave. You don't know what we heard. It's just one side."

I try to get around her, but she's annoyingly limber and blocks me every step I try to make.

"He's buying a woman, Kasia. What else do I need to know? This is the man that I'm falling in love with? A man who puts a dollar value on the life of a woman?" I shake my head as the words spill free of my mouth. Tears build up in my eyes.

She hugs me tight. "Ask him about it. Assuming you know what's going on will only cause a fight when there might not be a reason for one."

I pull free of her embrace. "And if he tells me he did buy her? That he's not happy with the stable but he's going to keep working it? What am I supposed to do then? Leaving him will only cause a fight with Roman."

She pinches her lips together. "From all the stories your brothers have told me about, I never pictured you as someone who gives up so easily."

"Gives up? I'm not giving up."

"Then why are you trying to run off?" she asks, folding her arms over her chest.

She's right, of course. Before I met Micah, I would shove through that door and demand answers. But that was before. I had nothing to lose then.

My chest clenches, keeping the air from my lungs. I close my eyes and slowly drag in a breath, concentrating on my lungs filling, stretching until I can't hold it anymore and let it out. I do this again before I face Kasia, my nerves somewhat settled.

"If he tells me he's going to help his father, I'll lose him," I say quietly. "I'll lose myself, too because I couldn't feel this way about a man like that. I just couldn't."

She stares at me for a long beat.

"But you're right. I don't give up, and I don't need him or my brothers to define what or who I am." Before any wind can fall from my sails, I spin on my heel and burst into Jakub's office.

All three sets of firm, angry eyes turn on me. But I won't be deterred.

"What is going on?" I demand.

"Lena, what are you doing back here?" Micah asks. "I told you to stay at the table."

"Contrary to what your family believes, I'm not some possession to be put on a shelf until ready for use."

Micah's jaw clenches. "Watch yourself, princess," Micah warns, his heated glare settles on me.

"Kasia, what's going on?" Dominik avoids me and asks his wife.

"You all disappeared, and we were just looking for you," she answers simply with a shrug but stands firm behind me.

"What were you talking to Niko about?" I settle my own glare on Micah. It's not nearly as fiery, I think; I haven't had the practice he's had. But I won't back down on this.

"An issue that's being resolved," Micah says, keeping me pinned to the floor with his gaze.

"What issue?"

"A business issue."

"Lena, leave it be for now." Dominik touches my arm, but I shove it away.

"Did you just tell Niko to buy a woman for your father's stable? Did you just give him the okay?" I ask. I'm not beating around the bush.

"Not exactly."

"You told him to buy a woman though."

"Yes. I did." He slides his hands into his pockets as though this is no big deal. He might as well have told Niko to pick up a pizza for dinner with the casual way he confesses his sin.

"Is that why you've been so busy this week? You've been helping your father stock up the stable?"

His eyebrow arches. "I've been working, Lena. You know that."

"That answers nothing." I turn to Jakub. "And what is your involvement with all this? Roman seeks to punish me because of you?"

Jakub stands straighter, his eyes darken. I've never seen him irritated before, at least not with me, but now that I have, I'm not sure I like it.

"Don't put any of this bullshit on my doorstep. I knew Igor years ago. I didn't have any sort of business dealings or friendship. He happened to be at the same party I was at, nothing more than that. If Roman wants to blame me for Igor getting a conscience, that's his problem."

I can't breathe, the air gets too thick. Sucking in a harsh breath doesn't help; it only gets stuck in my throat. I fist and unfist my hands, trying to work the anxiety from my chest and into my fingers. I need to breathe.

"Lena, you need to calm down." Micah steps to me. "Breathe, slow, baby, breathe slow."

I jerk away from him. His tenderness comes from a black soul. One that puts no value on a woman. He's his father's son.

It would have been better if he'd just left me in the stable. Having a happy ending dangling in front of me and then ripping it away is worse. So much worse.

"Lena, calm down." Dominik crowds me, too.

I shove away from all of them as tears roll down my cheeks.

"I hate you," I say to Micah with a shaking voice. It's the best I can do. There's a clog in my chest that's not letting anything else out. "I truly hate you."

"Lena." He reaches for me, intent on grabbing me, but I'm not sticking around. I'm done being the pawn in this game of men.

"No." I turn and run out of the room and down the hall. I hear the office door open and fast steps behind me, but it only makes me run faster.

I get outside the club, past the bouncer, and eye an Uber pulling up to the curb. Two women step out and as soon as they're clear, I jump in and lock the door.

"Hey. You have to use the app for a pickup. I can't just take you," the driver argues with me.

Micah rushes out of the club, looking up and down the street for me. Then his pitch black eyes land on mine, his jaw snaps closed, his eyes narrow.

"I'll pay you twice your fee, just get me away from here," I say.

He follows my gaze. "Yeah. Okay, sure." The car shifts into gear, and he pulls out into traffic just as Micah reaches the car.

Once we're a block away, I turn back around and take a steady breath. I flick away the tears on my cheeks.

"Where do you need me to take you?" he asks.

I have nowhere to go. Nowhere he won't find me.

So, I head to the only place a woman with no options can find safety.

CHAPTER 24

ena

It's late by the time the Uber pulls up to the single family Victorian tucked away in the western suburb. Thankfully, I'd kept my purse with me, so I'm able to give him the fare without a problem and he happily takes the double payment.

The chill of the fall night descends on me as I climb the wooden steps. I've always favored these old Victorian houses. I step up onto the wooden porch that wraps around the house. Rocking chairs and patio benches are lined up along the house beside the large bay windows. It has a deep feeling of home with the warm orange and brown hues of the exterior paints.

I ring the bell. At this late hour the alarm system will have been enabled and I don't have the code with me. The last thing anyone inside needs or wants is the police showing up and bringing a lot of attention to the house.

The light just inside the door flickers on and the intercom fizzles to life.

"Can I help you?" chimes a familiar voice.

"Hi. It's Lena. I'm sorry it's so late, but I needed—" Before I finish explaining the door swings open and the porch door is pushed at me, letting me inside.

"Lena. Come in. Sorry, I couldn't see clear through the camera." Sandra, the night shift manager, greets me, shutting and locking the door behind me once I'm inside the main foyer of the house.

"The lighting isn't great on the porch," I comment.

Sandra smiles and folds her arms over her chest. She's already dressed for bed in a pair of pink and gray cotton pajamas.

"Kasia's not here tonight," she says.

"Oh, I know." I fiddle with my purse. "I'm sorry, this is weird, I just didn't really know where else to go. I just…" I'm stumbling like a moron over my words.

"Sandra, we need—" Niko steps into the front hall from the staircase. His words fail when he sees me standing with Sandra.

"Lena." His eyes harden. "What are you doing here? Is Micah with you?" He looks behind him, as though Micah would be able to hide behind my frame.

"No. I just, I was—what are you doing here?" I go on the offense.

"He brought a woman in this evening. Dr. Sanja is with her now." Sandra turns to Niko. "What do you need?"

"The doc is done, she needs fresh clothes. I didn't see any in the room you're putting her in," Niko tells her while keeping his stare on me.

"I was just getting them when the bell rang. I'll get them for her." Sandra takes a step but then turns back to me. "Do you need me?"

"No. No. I'm fine. Go on."

She gives a nod then jogs up the stairs to where the women have private rooms. The medical rooms are also upstairs and if Niko brought that woman here, she would be with the doctor.

"Is that the woman you bought for Micah?" I demand.

"Micah doesn't know you're here, does he?"

"Answer me." I clench my fist.

He pulls out his phone.

"Don't." I get to him before he finishes dialing and snag his phone.

"What are you doing?" He reaches over and snatches it right back from me. "What are you doing here?"

"Is the girl you bought for Micah upstairs?" I ask, raising my chin a fraction. He doesn't answer me; he's too busy typing away on his phone. Tattling probably.

I shove him to the side and hurry up the stairs to the medical room.

"Lena!" Niko's voice is sharp enough to reach up the stairs as I head toward the medical rooms at the end of the hall.

Niko's hurried steps mingle with my own on the wood flooring as I head to the exam room. He's right next to me when I push the door open.

A woman sits on the exam table. Her hair has been washed and brushed back from her face, and that's where my heart rips in two. Bruises line the right side of her jaw. Her left eyebrow has been stitched, but it's still an angry red. These aren't the worst of her injuries. The medical gown slips down her shoulder and badly healed scars litter her shoulders down her back.

She doesn't seem startled by my sudden intrusion. How often has this woman even had privacy? When she looks up at me, there's a deep sadness, mistrust raging in her eyes.

"Demetria, it's okay. This is Lena." Niko pushes past me from behind and goes to her at the table. He picks up her hand and holds it. "She's Micah's wife."

I step closer to the table, my stomach in knots imagining the horrors this woman has seen.

"Niko, what happened to her?" I ask.

"Here we go." Sandra walks in with a pile of clothing. Soft pajamas from what I can make out. "We'll have more for you in the morning," she says to Demetria and places the pajamas on the bed beside her.

"Thank you," Demetria whispers and picks up the clothes with one hand.

"I'll let you change." Niko puts her hand down.

"Are you leaving?" Demetria asks, panic clear in her voice.

Niko touches her cheek. "No. I'm going to be just outside the door. When you're ready just let me know. I'll help you to your room."

She gives a shaky nod.

"I'm going to talk with the doctor. Come get me if you need," Sandra says.

Niko nods. "I'll get her in bed. I'm spending the night outside her door. It will make her feel better. Micah was going to come in the morning but—" He pauses to give me a stern look. Obviously, I'm intruding and messing up everything. "He'll be here tonight instead."

Heat rushes over my face. I've misread everything. Micah wasn't putting this woman in the stable, he was saving her. The women in this house are here because they have nowhere else to turn, because they've been rescued from the likes of the Ivanov family, or they've escaped horrendous abuses. I'm here running away from a fight with my husband.

"I'm so sorry," I say quietly and leave the room. Once in the hall, a dark shadow falls over me.

Micah is here.

I tilt my head back to find his angry glare settling on me as he walks the last steps toward me.

"Micah. How'd you get here so fast?" I ask, momentarily confused.

"Tracker on your phone. Remember?" he says. That's right. I never made him take it off. Another wave of embarrassment washes over me.

"Stand right there, and don't move." He moves past me as Niko comes out of the room. "She's in there?"

"Yeah, the doc just finished. Broken ribs, bruises, cuts—he really fucked her up." Niko keeps his voice level, letting me hear the extent of her injuries.

"What did he say about Roman?" Micah asks, his jaw clenching as they talk.

"Exactly what we thought. Roman came to him, offered her. Micah, he didn't take a penny for her. He only wanted the prick to send him periodic videos and pictures of his work."

Micah's hands ball together. "Did you talk to her?"

"She told me a little. She was kidnapped and put in your father's stable. Igor removed her from it, hid her best he could from your father's auctions. After his accident, Roman found her."

"And he made her pay for what Igor wanted to do, what he started to do." Micah's voice dipped lower. "He gave her to that fucking monster because Igor no longer wanted to back expansion of the stable."

My throat clenches as the betrayal and pain flash in his eyes.

"I'm staying here for the night—to be sure she's all right and feels safe," Niko explains, but there's an undercurrent of protection that I haven't seen in him before. It's only been a short time, but Niko's usually aloof. This woman is important to him.

"Thank you," Micah says. "Igor would want you here with her in his absence."

"What are you going to do with Roman?" Niko's question lands with a virtual thud between them.

"First things first," he says and glances in my direction. My insides curl. I've fucked up. I've been selfish and untrusting.

Micah wouldn't do what I accused him of doing. Micah isn't like his father. He's ruthless and demanding, yes, but he's not a monster. He would never hurt an innocent.

"I'm done," a soft voice calls from the medical room.

"We'll talk tomorrow." Niko enters the room, closing the door firmly behind him, leaving only Micah and me in the hall.

When Micah turns his attentions on me directly, my breath catches.

"Let's go," he says, cupping my elbow and leading me toward the stairs.

I don't argue, or fight, or even hesitate in my step. I've been a complete idiot tonight. Micah will help make things right between us.

I only hope I'm strong enough to take it.

CHAPTER 25

 icah

It's one in the morning by the time we get home. Lena didn't speak in the car ride back from the Staszek halfway house, and the ride up in the elevator was just as silent. Now that we're home, she slithers down the hall to our bedroom.

Every click of my leather-soled shoes on the tile makes her body tense another fraction. She'll break in half if she lets herself get any more wound up.

When she ran from Jakub's office, my first instinct was to get her and drag her back inside. But as the car pulled away with her staring out the back, tears shimmering in her silver blue eyes, fear trickled over me. Did she really believe me capable of the things she accused?

Thanks to the tracker on her phone, I was able to get to her within minutes of her stepping out of that damn Uber. She's lucky she had her purse with her; what if she had nothing with her? How would she have paid the fee? What would have happened to her if she couldn't?

As I walk down the long hallway to our rooms, the whirlwind of emotions returns. I've had women run off on me before out of anger. A great dramatic ploy to get attention, but Lena isn't like that. She didn't want me finding her. That's why she went to the halfway house.

If I hadn't had the tracker on her, I probably wouldn't have thought to look there. At least not at first. The mess with Demetria already had my nerves on edge, along with my meeting with Roman this afternoon. Having my wife run off on me has only put the icing on an extremely bitter cake.

Lena's already unzipping her dress when I enter the bedroom behind her. I walk past her to my side of the bed and strip out of my suit, down to my slacks.

"Micah." Lena's voice is soft, submissive even. When I look at her, there are tears again, dancing on the brim of her eyelids.

I fold my arms over my bare chest. I hadn't planned to talk with her yet. Not until the rawness of the evening wears away, but she looks damn pitiful.

"Micah, I'm sorry." She fiddles with her fingers. The dress has been quickly replaced with a thigh-length pajama shirt. I'd teased her about the casual nightgown when she'd worn it the first time. I don't feel like teasing right now.

"For what?" I say, unable to keep the edge from my voice.

She blows out a breath. "A lot of things." She takes in a shaky breath and holds it before letting it out.

Once she has her bearings, she continues.

"I should have asked you what was happening earlier. I shouldn't have assumed you were doing what I accused you of just from an overheard conversation. And I shouldn't have run away like that." Her apology is sincere and heartfelt. The little shudder of her breath tears away a layer of my anger.

"I asked you to trust me. You said you could do that," I remind her. The bed being between us is the only thing keeping me from pulling her to my chest. Seeing the sadness in her, the regret, it's painful.

"I know." She nods. "And I do trust you, or at least, I'm trying to."

"Then explain what happened tonight."

Her full lips pull down into a deep frown. "I messed up. You were so tense after you met with Roman this afternoon, and then when I heard you on the phone with Niko—I made an assumption."

I stare at her, taking in the remorse, the sweetness of her truth and an overwhelming sense rushes over me.

I love this woman.

And with that newsflash, the anger washes away, leaving me only with a sense to protect her. Even from herself.

"You've spent your entire life hearing only bits and pieces of things because your brothers and father have sheltered you. And I'm doing the same." I rub the back of my neck. "I want to protect you, to keep you from seeing the fucked-up world we live in. Because there are monsters out there, Lena. Worse than my father, and I don't want you exposed to them. Ever."

"I can handle the monsters, Micah." She glides around the bed, settling in front of me. "So long as I have you by my side." A soft pink tints her cheeks, and her eyes fall to my chin.

A feather could push me over after her words sink into my heart.

"You mean that, don't you?" I ask, still skeptical. How can a woman with such purity and strength have such feelings toward a man like me? At every turn she's followed her own path, even when it meant deceiving and hiding her true self from her family. I've done nothing but follow where I was told to go by my father. Responsibility to my family name led me by the nose through my entire life.

But I would risk it all, break through the noose around my neck if it meant protecting her.

"I do, Micah. I'm sorry I was such a brat tonight. I shouldn't have run away like that, and I shouldn't have assumed anything when I heard you talking."

"Considering my family businesses, and your experiences with them, I don't think it was such a far stretch of the imagination." I can concede that much on her behalf. My fingers itch to touch her silky-smooth skin, but once I do, I won't be able to stop myself.

"But you're not your father." She sits on the bed and looks up at me. "You're a good man, Micah. You saved that woman tonight."

Using my fingertips, I push the hair from her face and tuck it behind her ear. "Demetria was the woman my brother saved. Right before he died, he fell for her and took her from the stable before Roman could sell her. But Roman found out, and after Igor's death he hunted her down and sold her to the worst man he could find. Niko's been quietly searching for her since, but Roman wouldn't divulge who the buyer was. Niko was finally able to find her."

Sadness touches her eyes. It makes my stomach ache to see it, but she has too big of a heart not to be empathetic to Demetria's plight.

"He never told you about her?"

I clench my jaw. Igor and I never had a strong relationship. He'd been groomed from birth to take over for my father when the time came, while I was put on the back burner. Igor had his confidants, but I wasn't one of them.

"Igor and I weren't close."

"Do you think it's possible your father hurt Igor because of Demetria?" she asks, but there's hesitation there. It's a dangerous question.

"No." I shake my head. "Roman had other issues with Igor. But he wouldn't have killed him for them. He would have tossed him to the side and made me next in line. Sending Igor into exile after spending his entire life waiting for his time in the sun would have been a harsher punishment than death."

Though if Igor felt for Demetria what I feel for Lena, I'm not sure that's so true.

She picks up my hand and brings it to her cheek, leaning into my palm. Such fragility and strength mingled together with her simple gesture. "I really fucked up."

I chuckle. "And now you're adding bad language to the list."

When she turns her gaze up to me, there's uncertainty lingering in her stare. It's as though she wants to say something, confess something—but is holding back. Maybe it's the same thing I'm keeping to myself but analyzing all of that will take time. And right now, I have a naughty wife to deal with.

She lets go of my hand and gets up from the bed, heading around the footboard.

"Where are you going?" I ask her.

She points to her pillow. "To bed?"

I laugh. "Do you really think that's how this plays out?"

Her smile fades, as well as her confidence. "I already apologized, Micah."

I nod. "You did, that's right. Do you think my goal when I punish you is to make you sorry? All that does is make you sorry you got caught, not regretful of your actions."

She tugs at the hem of her nightshirt.

"You ran away tonight, Lena. You got in a cab and took off. Do you really think I'm letting you get into bed before you pay the consequence?"

She looks away, as though she can ignore the situation. But there's something else in her expression. Relief.

Lena

Whatever Micah is planning, it can't be worse than the heavy regret suffocating me. It's more than just the way I acted at the club or running away from him that's leaving this ache in my chest. It's the pure disappointment written all over his features when he saw me at the halfway house. The dead silence that built between us in the car on the way home. The fear that I'd made everything so bad, we'd go back to square one.

As much as I didn't want this marriage, now that we're in the thick of it, I don't share the same anger about it. I may never be loved by Micah, but I know he'll respect me.

"You took the evening from me, princess. Your behavior stole the night," he says while stalking his way around the bed toward me. He unbuckles his belt, making my ass clench at the prospect of what is to come.

"I know." I won't argue. I'll take what he gives me and wipe the slate clean. And tomorrow, things can go back to how they were.

"So now—" He reaches out to me and shoves me to my knees. Grabbing my hair in his fist, he yanks my head back. "I'm going to take from you, and you're going to be a good girl and deal with it."

With his free hand, he reaches into his unzipped pants and pulls out his thick cock. Slowly he strokes himself until a bead of pre-cum rests at the tip.

"Open that pretty mouth, Lena, and keep it open." He holds the head of his dick at my lips. I'm not stupid enough to pretend this is going to be easy. This is not better than an ass whipping with his belt. He'll be sure of it.

As soon as my mouth opens, he shoves his cock past my lips, down down down until he hits the back of my throat.

Instinctively, my throat clenches and I start to gag, but he holds me firmly.

"Breathe, princess. Swallow me down," he orders, tugging on my hair to keep my attention where he wants it.

I plant my hands flat on his thighs to brace myself, nothing more. There will be no pushing away from this, Micah will take what's his, and I can't stop him.

I don't even want to.

Finally, my throat relaxes, and he slips further down. I'm able to swallow again and keep from gagging.

"Good, princess," he coos and pulls back from my mouth. Never leaving completely but gives me enough space to take in a breath. It's a minuscule break though, before I can steady my breathing, he's pumping back into my mouth—fucking my face with as much fever as he fucks my pussy.

I'm already soaking my panties with his roughness and his power.

"Fuck, princess. Yes. Just like this." He holds my face on both sides and pushes me back until my head is against the bed. I have nowhere to go. I'm simply his vessel. His little fuck toy.

My clit twitches at the thought, but I don't dare touch myself.

Over and over again he pumps into my mouth, down my throat while I struggle for breath. After several strokes, he slows, letting me take a gasp. Tears leak down my cheeks, but he's not swayed by them.

"Bad girl tears don't run in sweet little lines like this." He smears them across my cheeks. "Better." He groans, then thrusts forward again.

Spit collects at the edges of my lips, spilling down my chin, but still, he doesn't stop.

His balls tighten, his strokes are slower, deeper. He's going to explode down my throat. I curl my hand around his balls, gently cupping and massaging him. The animalistic howl he lets loose tells me I did right.

"Fuck. Fuck." He moves his hand from my head to the bed and leans more into me. Another stroke, then another until he stills. Hot streams of cum shoot and spurt into my mouth, down my throat, over my tongue. I swallow as quickly as I can, and each constriction of my throat earns a muffled groan from him.

"Hold still, baby." He eases his cock from my mouth, then tips my chin up. "You've made a mess of yourself." He grins down at me and just like that, in that moment his disapproval washes away.

"Can I have a towel?"

He yanks off his t-shirt and wipes my chin and mouth clean. As he squats in front of me, he searches my face.

"You're not to touch that pretty pussy of yours tonight, Lena. You'll go to sleep hungry for my release, do you understand me?"

"I understand, Micah."

"Good." He kisses me gently. "Let's get to bed. I have an early morning." In one movement, he sweeps me into his arms and lifts me from my knees. I'm dropped into the bed with a bounce.

Once we're both in bed, beneath the covers, he snakes his heavy arm around my middle and drags me to him. There hasn't been a night since he's brought me to his bed that I've gone to sleep without his embrace.

I may never have his love, but I can live with this much from him.

I'll have to.

CHAPTER 26

Micah

I haven't had dinner with Lena in three nights. Between her volunteer time at the Staszek house and my working on the expansion of the restaurants, we've had no time together. We've fallen into a routine of sips of coffee between bites of breakfast as we get ready for our days.

These damn ledgers I'm staring at can wait. I grab my phone to text her that I'll meet her at home for dinner, but the door to my office bursts open and Roman stomps inside. I put my phone down and prepare myself for whatever storm he wants to bring in with him.

"Here you are. Of course, tucked in the back office of your restaurant instead of doing what I asked of you." Roman slams the door closed.

"What did you ask of me?" I stand up from my chair and fold my arms over my chest.

"You have invested all of your time into the restaurants. Into your dance clubs. Not one minute have you spent on the Ivanov businesses!" He points a shaky finger at me.

"The Ivanov businesses include my restaurants and my clubs. I'm not doing anything you didn't already know about. I told you I don't think expanding the stables is a good idea. We need more legitimate businesses, so the other avenues of our revenue are easier to filter." This conversation is so damn old cobwebs grow from it.

"Nothing I didn't know about?" His lips curl inward as he asks. "Demetria? You told me about her, did you?"

I leave emotion from my expression. It's one of the first things you learn growing up in my family. Never expose your true thoughts.

"Demetria was a private situation. It had nothing to do with you or the Ivanov businesses."

The information was also kept closely guarded. Two people other than me knew about Demetria. Finding her and extracting her had been Niko's doing, his secret self-imposed mission since the death of my brother. He wouldn't ruin all of that by telling Roman.

"Ah." He nods, but it's a farce. This calmness he's trying to portray is just the buildup until he unleashes his fury. "So, going behind my back to collect a woman who ruined your brother has nothing to do with me. Nothing to do with our family?"

"She didn't ruin Igor. He had opinions. You just didn't agree with them." I hold my ground. This man before me, seething and ready to throw a toddler-worthy tantrum is not the fire-breathing father I grew up with. He's laced with self-doubt and riddled with paranoia.

"Igor never would have even thought of going against me without her in his ear."

"He wasn't against you. Neither am I. He didn't want you doubling down on the stables. But it doesn't really matter now, though, does it? Igor's not here." I slam my fist into my desk. "He's not here. I am. I am your son, the one you keep touting as your heir. The one you say you want to take over the business when you retire, but you refuse to listen to anything I say."

"Because you want to take our family out of the business I've grown. The businesses that have proven profitable and can bring us even more money, more power. We are within grasp of having more control of this city and with that we can do whatever we want."

"The business streams that make a profit and keep the costs and risks low aren't being questioned. But your obsession with the fucking stable. For what? So you can get your cock sucked off at your whim?"

His jaw snaps shut, and irate red covers his face, but I'm not done yet.

"It's not profitable. Not anymore. And if you double down on it, it will cost us money. Let the other families chase their money with the girls. We have solid lines that make us twice as much, and the legit businesses not only increase our profits, but give us a shield." I march around my desk. No more hiding behind the shade of my brother. No more tiptoeing around my father's bullshit. If I'm to lead this family, I can't allow his temper tantrums to sway my actions. "You do what you want with the stable, but I won't work on it anymore.

And my men won't either." He has his own guys, but he's counted on my crews do some of his dirty work. He'll have to bring up his own ranks now.

"You think to tell me what is going to happen in my family?"

I shake my head. "No. You do what you think is best. I'll keep running the legitimate business side, and the other streams. You take the stable. Unless you'd like to retire altogether?"

There are men loyal to my father who would gladly cut off my head if given the direction, but I have more. I don't rule my men with fear, I rule with confidence and leadership. I won't ask anyone to cross lines here though; this is still the Ivanov family. And Roman will be the head until he chooses otherwise.

"Retire?" He says the word as though someone just shit in his mouth. "Why would I do such a stupid thing?"

"Because you're obsessed with a business that's dead. Because you can't see what's best for the family anymore, you only see what you want."

I half expect one of his guys to come through the door and shoot me. Men don't survive talking to Roman Ivanov the way I am.

He stares at me, the color fading on his cheeks until he's back in control of his anger. With a deep breath, he straightens his shoulders.

"I had a feeling you'd feel this way, Micah." The sneer in his voice lessens my confidence that I'm not about to get my ass handed to me.

"I'm only asking you to be logical."

He pulls out his phone and taps out a text message. After he puts it back in his inside pocket, he turns his twisted grin on me. "Why do you boys make me do things to you that will hurt you?"

Dread runs through my veins. "What the fuck does that mean?" I demand.

He shrugs and heads for the door.

"What did you do?" I grab my phone from my desk.

"You're as compromised as your brother was. I waited too long to get rid of the problem for him, but with you, I'm taking action faster."

I dial Lena's phone and press the phone to my ear. She's at home. She's safe there.

The phone rings and rings.

When the call goes to voicemail, I look back at the door. My father's gone.

I dial the phone again.

More ringing.

Voicemail.

Sweat breaks out on my brow. Maybe she's in the bathroom. Maybe she left her phone in the other room. Maybe she just doesn't hear it.

No matter what excuse I tell myself, the ice skating down my spine won't go away.

I'm out the door before the next ring of her phone, and in my car before the voicemail picks up.

If he touched a single hair on her head, I'll kill him myself.

CHAPTER 27

ena

A sharp throb in my temples wakes me from a restless sleep. As my eyes flutter open, a bright light makes me close them again.

I focus on the noise surrounding me. A deep laugh comes from far away. Metal clanks against a cement floor somewhere behind me. The shrill cry of a woman pleading sends ice coursing through my body.

I'm in the stable again. But not in the private room they had me in last time. There's a draft blowing against me as I lie on a metal slab. My wrists are bound to it, my ankles as well. I work my eyes open, turning my head to the side—away from the light shining down on me.

It's an open room, underground I think from the chill and the concrete floors and walls. No windows.

A metal door slams after another woman cries. There's a hallway. I must be in the main room of the stable. Tugging at the bindings on my wrists and ankles does no good. They're medical grade. The Ivanovs have experience with this; they aren't going to use something flimsy like tape.

"She's in the medical room," a dark voice says from behind me. Okay, so that's where I am. I guess that explains the metal table.

"Did you start yet?"

I freeze at the sound of that voice. I know it, I know him.

What is Dimitri doing here?

My mouth is dry, my throat clenched tight with fear. What are they going to start? Why am I here? Where is Micah?

"Just got the message from Roman. Now we can start," the unfamiliar voice says.

"Need some help?"

"No. I got this. Maybe you should get out of here. Just in case Micah catches wind. You don't want him to find out about you."

Dimitri laughs.

I try to twist my head around, to get a clear picture of them as their voices get louder, they move closer, but I fail.

"Micah's not dangerous. Roman's gonna cut him loose, he'll have no power. I'll still carry the Ivanov name. Once my uncle gets rid of him, I'm next in line. He'll be kissing my ass for protection from the rest of the family."

"We don't know that for sure. But..." He pauses. Their footsteps stop just behind me. "Considering Roman sent Micah's little princess down to me, I'm guessing you're probably right."

A hand touches my hair and I jerk against my bindings. My scream is muffled by the rag stuffed in my mouth; another is tied around my head.

"Shh, it's okay, sweetheart." The dark voice comes closer to me. The scent of stale cigar and liquor envelops me as he puts his lips against my ear. "I'll take good care of you."

I yank harder on the cuffs and wiggle hard enough to make the table sway.

"Enough!" He slams his hands down on either side of me on the table.

Dimitri laughs. "She's not as weak as you think, Viktor. Keep your eye on her."

Anger rises up in my chest. How can Dimitri betray Micah this way? They've been friends, allies, since childhood. What could cause him to turn his back so readily on that?

"I have a meeting with Christian Kaczmarek. I'll leave you to your work." Dimitri pats my cheek. "You be a good girl now for Viktor. He's going to be gentle, so long as you behave. If you get stubborn, he'll have to punish you. And not the way you like." His thick Russian accent gives the threat a more dangerous tint. My stomach rolls at what he could mean.

"Don't go anywhere, princess. I'll be back." Viktor touches my shoulder. Hearing the endearment that's become so commonplace for Micah to use coming out of that traitor's mouth heats my blood.

"You think it's a good idea, getting back into business with another Polish family? We have our own we can work with,"

Viktor says as the two of them walk away. Their shoes tap against the cement as they go; it's the only sound in the room.

"After you're finished with Lena, there's a good chance her father will bring war down on us. Roman's preparing an alliance with the Kaczmareks to protect us."

"Well, I'm sure the old man knows what he's doing."

A door opens and shuts.

For a moment, I think I'm alone again. The tightness in my chest eases enough for my breathing to come easier. But then the footsteps start again, along with a high-pitched squealing sound. Wheels rolling over the smooth cement.

Viktor comes into view, rolling a medical tray in front of him. With only a quick glance I see equipment. Similar to what my gynecologist uses during an exam, but there are more tools on his tray.

My breath catches again. Tears burn my eyes, rolling down my cheeks.

I yell through my gag. But it doesn't matter.

There's no one here to hear me, even if I could get the sound to escape the cloth.

"Relax, Lena." Merriment dances in his voice. I look down the length of my body and find him standing at my feet. He kicks a stool closer, then sits down, his head now level with me. "I'm only going to remove your implant."

My implant. He's removing my birth control.

I wiggle hard against the binds, making the table rock, but he's quick to steady it.

"If you keep doing that, I will paralyze you for the procedure. You'll be completely awake and aware, but you won't be able to move. Which works nicely for me. But if I have to go through all that, there will have be something in it for me. How does a nice fucking sound?"

A whimper escapes from behind my gag. He's not threatening, he's promising. And from the bulge in his pants, I'd say he's enjoying the prospect of being able to do just that.

I lie still and wrap my fingers around the edge of the table. Gripping the side is all I can do, it's the widest range of motion I have.

"There. Better." He sits back on the stool and turns a crank beneath me. My legs spread until I'm completely open to him. Hot tears roll down my temples, pooling in my hair, running into my ears. There's a dark water stain on the ceiling above me, just above the hanging light. I fixate on it, putting all my focus on it and try to count my breaths.

"Don't worry, Lena. No one is going to hurt you unless you make them." Latex gloves snap against his wrist.

I take a deep breath in, one, two, three. Then out again, slow and easy.

"Once we get this implant out of you, you'll go into the breeding room. There we'll have a few different men mount you until you're pregnant. Once you're pregnant, we'll return you to Micah."

His fingers are on me and my body clenches. This can't be happening. It can't. I can't breathe. My chest is too heavy, there's too much weight on me.

"We'll see how much loyalty Micah shows you when he realizes you're carrying another man's baby. Divorce isn't an option, I'm sure you know. And Roman won't allow Micah to abandon you, so, even though he'll be cut out of power, he'll still be at the mercy of his father. And you'll be at the mercy of your husband."

No matter where I try to focus my mind, put my attention, his words break through. Killing me would hurt Micah for a little while but making him raise someone else's child, making him look at me every day and know what was done to me will break him forever.

With the way my legs are tied to the table, I can't even push my knees together. If I fight him, I have no doubt he'll do as he promises, but if I don't try to get away the next part will be even worse.

Raped. Repeatedly. For how many days, by how many people?

I try to suck in air, but the gag is stopping me. My mind swirls, my chest clamps. I can't breathe. I can't think. My stomach rolls as though I'm doing a nosedive on a roller coaster.

"Get the fuck away from her."

Micah.

I hear Micah.

I thrash my head from one side to another, trying to get the gag loose enough to let in air. I'm going to pass out. I can't breathe.

"Micah."

"Back away."

The stool hits the floor. Where's Viktor?

Black edges into my vision.

"Your father—"

A gunshot rings out, echoing in the small area. Loud ringing blares in my ears. I start tugging on my bindings again. I need to breathe. I need the gag out.

"Lena!" Micah's face hovers directly over me. "Breathe, baby, breathe." He works the gag out of my mouth, letting it hang around my neck. I spit out the balled-up rag from inside, and take the deepest breath I've ever taken.

"Breathe with me." He captures my face with his hands. Men run into the room and down the corridors. They shout commands at each other, but Micah's dark eyes have my full attention.

He counts for me.

"In, Lena, breathe in. That's good. One. Two. Three. Good girl." He wipes my cheeks. "Now out, slow, no, slow down, Lena, slow breaths." He counts down again for me and within a few tries I catch my breath and the swirling stops in my head.

A sob breaks free finally.

"Let me get you untied." He's quick unbuckling the belts from my wrists. "Okay, okay, let me help you." He wraps his arm around my back as I sit up. I'm still in my blouse and skirt from earlier, but they've removed my panties.

Micah pushes the legs of the table back together and unbuckles the restraints. Before I can swing my legs around to the side, he has me up in his arms, carrying me against his chest.

"Don't look," he tells me when I try to see over his shoulder. Viktor lies on the floor; a puddle of blood slowly spreads out around him.

I should have listened. My stomach twists again, so I close my eyes. I'm not cut out for so much blood.

"Micah." Niko rushes up to us as Micah takes me to the main entrance. "What do you want done with the other men?"

"They belong to my father. They brought my wife here, Niko. What do you think is to be done with them?" Micah's voice is so cold, so distant, a shiver runs through me.

"I'll see it done."

"Every woman down here is to be brought to the Staszek house," Micah orders.

"Micah," I say, my throat raw.

"Shh, Lena, rest."

"No." I push off his chest and wiggle my way out of his arms. He puts me on my feet and glares down at me.

"I'm taking you home, Lena. Niko and my men will see that the girls here are taken care of." He thinks I'm going to argue about the girls.

"Dimitri."

He raises his brow. "What about him?"

"He took me."

His frown deepens. "I know."

"He's not here. He went to meet with Christian Kaczmarek." I swallow against the dryness of my throat. My head pounds, and although my breathing is coming easier, my chest aches.

Micah exchanges a look with Niko. "He's been dealt with, Lena," he says to me, cupping my shoulders beneath his warm hands. "He's been feeding my father information about you and about me for weeks."

I blink back a new round of tears.

"They were going to—" My voice cracks beneath the weight of what could have happened if Micah hadn't arrived.

"They won't ever touch you again. I'll explain everything later. Right now, I'm taking you home." He runs the back of his knuckles across my cheek, wiping away a rolling tear. "I'll carry you if you can't walk. The drug they gave you makes you woozy," he reminds me. It's not the first time I've had this drug.

"I can walk," I say quietly watching Nikko head down the corridors to where the girls are being kept. "But I think I'd like it if you carried me."

A soft smile breaks out on his lips, and he swoops me into his arms again. I wrap my arms around his neck and snuggle into his chest beneath his chin. Inhaling the spiced scent of his aftershave warms me; it sends a signal to my body that I'm safe. I'm all right.

Micah will keep me safe.

CHAPTER 28

icah

Lena's asleep on the couch. I tried to get her to lie down in bed, but she insisted she wanted to rest in here. I'm getting soft. I should have put her to bed anyway.

I could have lost her today. The reality of that hits me harder than any bullet could. They weren't planning to kill her. If they had succeeded in the torment they had planned, I could have lost the Lena I know.

The Lena I love.

My heart aches and soars with the notion of loving this woman. Loving her brings danger; she can be used against me—again.

I move from the armchair to the coffee table, sitting close enough to her that I can brush the messy locks of hair from her face. Her cheeks are still puffy from crying; even after she showered, I can see the tracks of her tears.

They didn't hurt her. I try to console my anger with that fact, but it's bullshit. Her scars aren't physical. They're inside, buried, and they're all my fault.

"Micah, they're here," Niko informs me a mere second before the room is invaded by the Staszek family. Joseph settles a hateful glare on me as he walks to his sleeping daughter.

I get up from the coffee table and ward them all off.

"No. Let her sleep." I stop Kasia and Jakub before they can reach her while Dominik and Joseph keep to the doorway.

"Let's go in the kitchen." I usher them out of the living room and down the hall.

"Let me sit with her. If she wakes up, it's better if she's not alone." Kasia stops just outside the kitchen.

I nod in agreement. The last thing I want is Lena to be frightened in her own home.

"Thank you," I say and Kasia hurries back to the living room.

"What happened?" Joseph demands as soon as we're alone.

"My cousin betrayed me. He helped my father take Lena." I lean a hip against the kitchen island.

"I know that," Dominik snaps. "But is she okay? Has a doctor looked her over?"

I level my stare on his. "Yes. To both questions. I got there before they could do anything to her."

Dominik's glare softens a fraction. From what I've heard of his relationship with his wife, he can relate to tonight's events.

"I never should have agreed to this marriage," Joseph steams. "I was stupid. Selfish." Pain wrinkles his features. He gave his only daughter to my family. My father had already kidnapped her once; Joseph knew the dangers. But he wanted peace, and he'd given her in exchange for it.

"She's safe," Jakub speaks up. "She's safe with Micah. He found her before anything bad happened. He won't let his family hurt her."

Joseph frowns. "We don't know that. Roman will go after him now; that makes her a target."

"Roman is being taken care of," I assure him. Nausea rolls into my belly because it's the truth. "He won't be an issue by morning."

Joseph perks up. "What does that mean exactly?"

I push off the countertop. I'm breaking a code by informing them, but they are Lena's family and deserve to know the truth.

"My father got in over his head with the stable. His partners back in Russia demanded more than he could give, but he continued making promises. He continued taking payments for girls he didn't have to sell."

"That's why he pushed for expansion." Niko steps into the kitchen. "Lena's awake. Kasia's sitting with her."

"So, what are you doing now?" Dominik asks.

"His partners are tired of waiting, and Roman doesn't have the inventory he promised." I shrug. "Like I said, by morning Roman won't be an issue."

There should be a sense of dread, of worry or anger at the prospect of what torture they will put my father through before they end his miserable existence. Instead, relief floods me. He can't hurt Lena, and I don't have to walk behind him cleaning up his messes anymore.

"He's tarnished my family's name in this city and back in Russia. The stable is closed for good," I announce, keeping my attention on Dominik. "That should make your wife happy."

"And yours," Dominik responds.

I smile. "Yes, Lena will be as well. The peace between our families stands firm. The territory lines will revert back to where they were before my father's fight with your family. Everything goes backward."

Stress elevates across Joseph's features.

"Lena remains my wife." I point a finger at him. "I'm not giving her up."

Dominik huffs a laugh. "No one suggested otherwise."

"Does she know all this?" Jakub asks.

I shake my head. "No. I've been working on things the past few weeks, but until I knew for certain I didn't want her to worry. I did not know Dimitri was working with my father. But I should have suspected."

Dimitri's betrayal blindsided me. Though looking backward, I see the red flags. I had believed we were on the same side, that my father and I were on the same side. Both were working against me, and I missed it.

"What of Roman's men? Those that are loyal to him?" Joseph asks, his voice lowered.

"There will be a clean house in the Ivanov family by morning." I won't say another word on the matter. It a cleansing that's necessary but not one I enjoy. Good men will be put on the outside of their lives, while sour souls will be ended.

"So, this is where the meeting is." Lena walks into the kitchen with a wobbly smile. She's pulled her hair into a loose ponytail on top of her head. The sweatshirt and yoga pants she's wearing makes her look more comfortable than I'm sure she is.

"You should be lying down," I say, walking to her. She waves me away.

"I'm fine, Micah. I'm mostly just a little tired from the sedative they gave me." She brushes past me. "I'm thirsty though."

"Get her some water," Joseph demands and goes to his daughter. "Are you hurt? Does your head hurt? What hurts?"

It's the first time I've seen him gush over her. The night of the arrangement, he barely gave her a glance. He's been distant since the wedding, too. But this looks natural, sincere. I wonder how many nights he's laid awake worrying about his little girl, but pride and code made him stay away.

Lena puts on a brave smile. "I'm fine, Dad. Truly. I'm okay. Nothing hurts," she says, but her eyes are slightly narrowed. The lighting in here pains her, but she's not going to let on. She'll brave it out.

"Niko, there's ibuprofen in the bathroom of my office. Get three." I send him while she's still convincing her family she's not hurt.

"The girls." Lena turns to Kasia as memory invades her. "From the stable."

Kasia nods. "There were twenty-five and they've all be brought to the Staszek house. Dr. Sanja is taking good care of them. They're safe, Lena."

Lena's shoulders drop with relief.

Niko returns with the pills and gives them to Lena. She tries to deny them at first, but she catches my glare and concedes.

"Well." Joseph straightens his back. "You need rest, and we're keeping you up."

"I'll stay so I can—" Kasia starts.

"No, Kasia." Dominik grabs her hand. "You'll come home. Micah has this under control, and if Lena needs us, she'll call."

"I will. I'll call," Lena promises as she downs the last pill.

I step out of the way as her family files past, giving her a kiss or a hug before disappearing down the hall with Niko. We're left alone starting at each other. She averts her gaze from mine.

"You're hurting," I accuse softly.

"My head," she says and sinks into one of the island stools. "I'll be okay. It's just from the drug, like I said."

She's right, but that doesn't cool my anger.

"I should have known it was Dimitri." I slide closer to her. "He's been asking more questions lately than usual. Volunteering to watch out for you. I thought he was just getting lazy and liked lounging around while you worked."

She lifts her eyes to mine. "I didn't think anything of it when he told me I needed to go with him. He said you wanted me, but when I tried to call you, he took my phone. The next thing I knew I was waking up on that table." Tears shimmer in her eyes.

Instinct has me reaching out to her, touching her cheek. "I have no right to ask for your forgiveness. I put you in danger. I didn't protect you."

She furrows her brow. "This wasn't your fault, Micah. This was evil men doing evil things." She flicks away a tear with her fingers and leans forward into me.

I wrap my arms around her, holding her tight to me.

"When I was lying there and Viktor told me what he was going to do, I was so scared." She looks up at me. "Not of the pain, but of losing you. How could you ever come to love me if they had succeeded?"

I cradle her face in my hands. "Listen to me, Lena." I lean into her. "I love you now and I will love you forever. It's not a matter of if or when. Do you understand me?" Another tear falls and I catch it with my thumb, wiping it away.

"And if he had succeeded?"

"It wouldn't have changed anything. I would still love you." I kiss her soundly, pressing against her hard. I don't want her to ever think she isn't my entire world, because she is. There is no sunrise without her, no heartbeat that matters without her next to me. She needs to know that, she needs to feel it in her bones the same way I do.

"I love you, Micah," she whispers when I break the kiss.

"I know, Lena." I grin. "You're not as good at hiding your feelings as you think you are."

Her eyebrows raise and she smiles. "I'm too tired to argue with you."

"Hmm, I'll have to keep that in mind for the future."

She shakes her head with a laugh. "You're impossible."

"I try." I hug her to me again, kissing the top of her head and enjoy the feeling of her against me.

"The men at the stable?" she asks after moments tick by.

"Don't worry about that."

Lena pulls back and stares up at me. "No more keeping me in the dark, Micah. I don't need to know your business, but tell me what happened to those men, with your father."

I sigh. She's right. No more trying to protect her by keeping her at arm's length.

"The men at the stable have been dealt with and my father as well. He won't be an issue anymore."

She takes a deep breath. "He's dead?"

"If not already, he will be by morning," I assure her.

"I'm sorry."

"For what?" I can't imagine what she could possibly be apologizing for.

"He's your father," she says simply.

"No, Lena. He's just a man and he's gone."

"That means you're the head of your family now."

I nod. "Yes. It's going to be a very busy time for a while."

"The restaurants?"

"Everything. I need to get my family in order."

"I'll help, whatever you need, I'll help," she offers. When I can't imagine loving this woman any more, she pushes past the limit.

"You'll go to school. You'll follow your passions, and we'll work everything else out around it."

"Together."

I can't fight the smile pulling on my lips. "Yes, together."

"Since your father's not in charge, you could give me back. You could let me go." She's teasing.

"I don't think so, princess." Since she's well enough for joking, I yank her off the stool and up into my arms.

I carry her from the kitchen and head to our bedroom. Niko stands at the ready near the elevators. There's going to be a lot of changes coming in the next few days and until things settle, we'll be having men stationed in the house. I won't have Lena put in danger again.

As we pass through the sitting room of our suite, she hugs me.

"So you won't let me go?"

I drop her onto the bed and peel off my shirt.

"No, princess." I climb into bed, draping my body over hers and capturing her mouth in a deep kiss.

"I'll be keeping you, Lena."

She kisses me right back. "I didn't think it possible, but I know it now." She runs her fingertips over the scar on my jaw. "The best thing that's ever happened to me, Micah, is being kept by you."

CHAPTER 29

M*icah*

The overwhelming stench of rotting flesh greets me as I jog my way down the cellar steps. It's dark except for a single bulb swaying from the ceiling. The door I need is on the other side of the empty room.

Boxes and pallets have been discarded. Old stains of blood mark the concrete flooring. Neither of these things account for the stink of piss mingling in the air as I get closer to the door.

It's still early, the sun hasn't even kissed the sky yet, but I'm wide awake. I haven't slept. How could I with this monster still on the loose. Until I know it's done, that Lena is completely safe, and my future is completely within my grasp, I won't be able to relax.

I rap my knuckles on the door twice, and it opens immediately. Another dark room, but there's more light in here.

"Micah. I'm surprised you came." Milo Romanov, the head of the Romanov family, greets me with a handshake.

"It's my responsibility," I tell him as the door closes behind me. Two men stand guard, their arms folded over their chests.

"You're not here to put up a fight then?" Milo asks in a low tenor. He's fifteen years older than me, but the extra years have aged him twofold. Being in charge of his family has probably done him in.

Will I look so ragged and worn down in a few years?

"I'm here to take care of my business," I say. "Nothing's changed since we spoke last night."

He runs his tongue over the top row of his teeth. "You don't have to do this," he leans in and whispers.

When he moves, I get my first glimpse of the man hunched over in a chair. His hair is wild around his hanging head. Blood drips from his mouth onto his equally bloody legs. They've beaten him.

"Is he still breathing?"

Milo glances over his shoulder. "Yes."

I pull out my gun. "Good."

"Before you do this." Milo puts a heavy hand on my arm. "We should come to an understanding."

I raise my eyes to his, tensing my jaw as I take in his authoritative glare. Gently I pull away from his touch.

"The only understanding we need, Milo, is you have your family and I have mine. Our businesses don't depend on each other, and they never will."

His eyes narrow. After a long pause he gives a small nod. "I have no problem with that. I have other suppliers. The Ivanov family is out of the trade as far as the Romanovs are concerned."

"Good."

He steps back from me.

"I'll leave you to it."

As I approach the huddled, pathetic mess of a man, he lifts his head.

"Micah." He manages my name with a rough whisper. His good eye moves to the gun in my hand and his swollen lips spread into something like a smile. There's so much bruising and blood, it's not easy to look at him.

"You tried to hurt my wife." It's the only statement I can think. Remembering her tied down to that medical table, seeing the tears streaking her face, and hearing her gasp for breath while trying to fight off her anxiety has my blood heated again.

He turns his attention to Milo and his guards behind me. "You aren't here to save me."

"I won't let them kill you," I say, because it's my job. I won't allow the Romanovs to take his life. Bound by my family's code, I'd have to retaliate. The Ivanovs take care of their own.

I raise my gun, pointing it directly at my father's head. My hand is steady, my finger finds the trigger.

Like a rabid animal, my father needs putting down. He's a menace. A danger to my wife.

He looks away from me, bowing his head before me.

Lena will be safe.

I pull the trigger.

EPILOGUE

*L*ena

Six months later

"Micah, can't you yell at Niko later?" I place my hand on his thigh as Luka, our driver for the day, parks the SUV in front of Dominik's house.

Micah rattles off what I assume is a few more insults in Russian into his cellphone then hangs up.

"You're being grumpy," I chide him with a smile. He's been stressed. Handling the Ivanov businesses while trying to expand the legitimate side wears on him. "Trust Niko." I slide across the seat and climb out of the car. "He doesn't need his hand held at every turn."

Micah grabs my hand and squeezes. "And since when do you lecture me on behavior?"

My cheeks heat at the implication. There's still tenderness in my ass from this morning.

"Since you're taking your stress out on Niko."

He sighs as we reach the front door. "Once this restaurant opens, it will be easier."

"Things will never be easy, Micah. You're running two empires at the same time." I ring the bell.

"It will work out." He squeezes my hand again, a signal to drop the conversation as the door opens.

Kasia greets us with a wide smile and big hugs before leading us to the back of the house where the rest of my family is already hanging around the kitchen.

"Micah. Lena." My father smiles as he stuffs a cookie into his mouth. These family gatherings have become more difficult to schedule.

"Where's Jakub?" I ask, noticing my brother is missing.

Dominik waves at the back door. "On the porch. Something at the club needed his attention."

"Jakub is good with the management of the club." I hint, nudging Micah with my elbow. He raises an eyebrow at me, then goes over to the fridge to get himself something to drink.

"Lena. Do you think you can spend some time at the Staszek house this week? One of my volunteers had to cancel," Kasia asks while fixing a salad.

"Sure. I have a pretty easy week."

"Great."

Jakub slams the porch door when he returns.

"Hey. Watch the door," Dominik barks at him.

"Sorry," Jakub mutters.

"What's wrong at the club?" I ask, settling into one of the island stools.

"The new night manager I hired—" He cuts himself off and takes a deep breath. "Nothing. Just personnel issues."

Dominik rolls his eyes. "He hired the first woman he interviewed and then wonders why she can't manage her way out of a room with one door."

"Is she pretty?" I ask with a laugh.

Jakub flashes me a glare.

I laugh harder. "She is."

"I'm going to have to hire someone else."

"Just make sure you get someone you can trust." My father wags his finger at him. "And no one with drama. You need someone who keeps their nose on their own papers."

"I'll get someone," Jakub assures us then grabs a beer from the fridge. "When is dinner?"

Kasia looks at the oven. "An hour?"

Micah hands me a glass of wine.

"Micah. Your father's house is still for sale?" My father brings up the one subject that will put Micah in a sour mood. After we buried Roman, Micah put the estate up for sale, not wanting to step foot on the property again.

"Did you want to buy it?" Micah asks, thankfully keeping his tone somewhat light.

Dad laughs. "No, of course not."

Jakub's phone goes off again. "For fuck's sake. I'm getting a new manager tomorrow." He takes the call and stomps off into the living room to deal with the new drama.

Dominik hugs Kasia and whispers something into her ear that makes her blush.

"Lena." Micah nudges me. "You aren't jealous of that, are you?" he whispers into my ear and points toward my brother. "Because if you want me to make you blush up to your ears, just let me know. I think I can manage pretty well."

Just the prospect of what he might say has my face heated.

He chuckles. "Damn, I'm good."

I roll my eyes and take a sip of my wine. He is good. Damn good, but there will be no living with him if I let him get too big of an ego.

"You're impossible." I try to push him away, but he's being playful.

"I am, I agree." He kisses my temple. "And you wouldn't have me any other way."

He's right.

I hide my smile behind my wineglass.

"I need a drink," my father mutters and stalks out of the room. He's probably searching out Dominik's private stash.

"I don't think he likes seeing me touch you," Micah jokes.

"He's not the only one," Dominik says from the other side of the kitchen island.

"Well, if it upsets you, big brother…" I turn in my stool and grab Micah's shirt, pulling him down toward me as I reach up and kiss him.

"Such a damn brat," Dominik remarks.

Micah smiles down at me. "And I wouldn't have it any other way," he whispers.

The End

AFTERWORD

Stormy Night Publications would like to thank you for your interest in our books.

If you liked this book (or even if you didn't), we would really appreciate you leaving a review on the site where you purchased it. Reviews provide useful feedback for us and our authors, and this feedback (both positive comments and constructive criticism) allows us to work even harder to make sure we provide the content our customers want to read.

If you would like to check out more books from Stormy Night Publications, if you want to learn more about our company, or if you would like to join our mailing list, please visit our website at:

http://www.stormynightpublications.com

BOOKS OF THE MAFIA BRIDES SERIES

Taken by Him

Four years ago I signed a contract. Today Dominik Staszek came to collect what is his.

Me.

He is not a gentle man, and he will not be a gentle husband.

Not even on our wedding night. Not even my very first time.

Before we even spoke our vows I felt the sting of his belt on my bare bottom, but it was only once I was bound to his bed that I began to truly understand what it means to belong to him.

I am not just his bride. I am his completely.

BOOKS OF THE OWNED AND PROTECTED SERIES

Protecting His Pet

After her brother's life of crime is brought to a sudden end, twenty-two-year-old Kara Jennings fears she may be the next target of the men who killed him. It comes as a shock, however, when she is taken captive by a mysterious man who promises to keep her safe but quickly demonstrates that he will not hesitate to punish her in any way he sees fit if she disobeys him.

Devin Stringer is certain there is something important that Kara is refusing to share with him—something related to her brother's death—and he is fully prepared to be as firm as necessary to get her to tell him the truth, even if that means stripping her bare, spanking her soundly, and keeping her caged like a pet.

Despite her shame at being made to kneel naked at her captor's feet, eat from his hand, and surrender her body to him completely, Devin's dominance leaves Kara helplessly aroused and yearning for him to master her even more thoroughly. When he brings her to the edge of an intense climax only to leave her desperate and wanting, her need for him to claim her properly compels Kara to confess the secret her brother shared with her before his death. But will that information help Devin protect his beautiful pet or will it ultimately put her in greater danger?

Protecting His Runaway

After she uncovers her wealthy father's ties to a prominent Chicago crime family, twenty-four-year-old Addison St. Claire flees to a small town in Michigan where she hopes to start a new life. Things are not that simple, though, and she is quickly tracked down by a stern, handsome police detective who makes it clear that Addison will be coming with him whether she likes it or not.

Detective Trevor Stringer is none too pleased at being assigned to babysit a spoiled rich girl, but he is determined to keep Addison safe, even if that means taking her over his knee for a painful, humiliating bare-bottom spanking when her defiance puts her life at risk. Despite her protests, her body's response to his bold dominance makes it obvious that Addison is in need of a firm-handed man to keep her in line, and before long she is begging Trevor to claim her properly.

Over the coming days, Addison learns what it means to belong to a man who will not hesitate to strip her bare and punish her thoroughly whenever he feels it necessary. Whether she is pleading desperately for the release she has been denied after a hard spanking or writhing with pleasure more intense than she can handle as she is brought to one shattering climax after another, Addison is left with no doubt that she has been mastered completely. But when she discovers that Trevor has kept an important secret from her, will she ever be able to trust him again?

His Captive Pet

Aubree Stevenson isn't used to being ordered around, but then her efforts to bring down a dog fighting ring put her life in danger and she ends up in the protective custody of a stern, handsome former Marine.

Blake Turner is not a man to be trifled with, and he wastes no time in making it clear that Aubree will obey him or be punished. After she puts his word to the test, Aubree's bottom is bared for a painful, embarrassing strapping, and when she continues to defy her strict captor, she quickly discovers that he is prepared to take things much further. Soon enough, she finds herself stripped naked, outfitted with a collar and tail, and eating from Blake's hand like a well-trained pet.

To her dismay, Aubree's arousal grows more intense with every shameful display of forced submission. But even as he masters her body and claims her in every way, Blake must keep his captive pet safe from both her enemies and her own recklessness. Will he prove up to the task?

His Captive Kitten

After her efforts to track down her missing mother nearly get her killed, twenty-seven-year-old Julie Sampson ends up on the run, hiding out in a cabin with police officer John Hamish. Though Julie is used to fending for herself, John demands her absolute obedience while she remains in his custody, and she quickly discovers that her gruff, infuriatingly sexy protector will not hesitate to strip her bare and take a leather strap to her naked bottom when she defies him.

Determined to teach Julie to submit for her own safety, John decides to treat her as his pet, and the beautiful, headstrong young woman soon finds herself sleeping in a cage, wearing nothing but a tail, and learning the hard way that her master will not hesitate to show a sassy little kitty a better use for her mouth.

But even when she is punished in ways more shameful than she would have thought possible, Julie cannot deny her body's desperate need for John's stern dominance. When he takes her in his arms and claims her hard and thoroughly, she is left sore, spent, and satisfied, but can she bring herself to trust that no matter what, her master will never abandon his kitten?

Becoming His Pet

After she witnesses a mob hit, twenty-five-year-old Nora Santucci avoids becoming the next victim only due to the timely intervention of rough, battle-hardened ex-Marine Greg Turner. But when she tries to run, her rescuer takes matters into his own hands, making it very clear that he will not hesitate to tan her cute little backside if she doesn't start doing exactly as she is told.

Insisting that she won't be safe in the city, Greg brings his beautiful, feisty prisoner to his secluded hunting cabin, where he sets about getting the truth from her. When she lies one too many times about her connection to the man who was killed, Nora quickly finds herself bound, gagged, and sobbing as she is thoroughly and painfully punished, but even with the welts from her captor's cane crisscrossing her bare bottom, her intense, helpless arousal is undeniable.

Nora's desire only grows stronger when Greg informs her that from now on she will be his little pet, and soon she is blushing crimson as he brings her to a quivering climax in her cage. Wearing a tail and eating from a bowl on the floor merely increase her need for him, and by the time he claims her she has been made to beg for it more shamefully than she would have thought possible. But when the time comes to return to Chicago and Nora discovers that her trust in an old friend turns out to have been badly misplaced, will it end up costing Greg his life?

Training His Pet

Erika Devore is known for getting the stories nobody else can, but when she ends up on the wrong side of a mob boss she suddenly finds herself in the custody of a former soldier turned security contractor who has made it his business to keep her safe whether she likes it or not.

Dax Adams is determined to protect Erika, even if that means spanking her until she is sobbing every time her reckless defiance puts her in danger. But when she discovers that the cabin he has chosen as their hideout is part of a BDSM resort, Erika's intrigue and arousal are both obvious, and Dax decides that the best way to keep her occupied and obedient is to train her as his pet.

Though Dax gives Erika no choice in the matter, her body's response to his bold dominance is undeniable, and soon she is kneeling naked at his feet, blushing as she is fitted with a tail for the first time, and screaming in helpless pleasure as she is brought to one desperately intense climax after another. But when it is safe for her to return home, will that bring an end to her training?

MORE STORMY NIGHT BOOKS BY MEASHA STONE

The Mob Boss' Pet

My men grabbed Stephania Benzitto because my brother needed a doctor and I'd prefer to avoid the kind of questions I'd have to answer if we went to a hospital, but that's not why I kept her.

Stephania is kneeling at my feet wearing nothing but a leash, a collar, and the stripes of my belt on her beautiful bare bottom because I've decided to make her my pet, and a pet must be tamed.

She will be caged until she learns to obey. Then she will find out how good pets are rewarded…

MEASHA STONE LINKS

You can keep up with Measha Stone via her website, her Facebook page, and her Goodreads profile, using the following links:

https://meashastone.com/

https://www.facebook.com/measha.stone.5

https://www.goodreads.com/author/show/8364578.Measha_Stone

Made in the USA
Columbia, SC
13 May 2021